the GARFIELD show

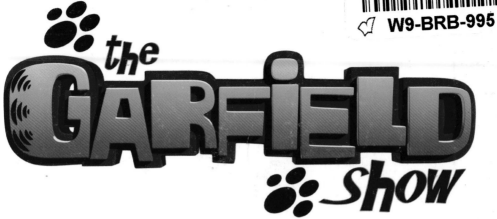

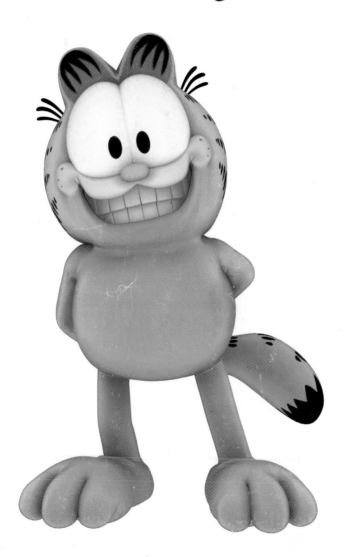

PAPERCUTZ™

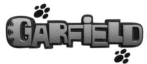

GARFIELD GRAPHIC NOVELS AVAILABLE FROM PAPERCUTZ™

GARFIELD
FISH TO FRY
& Co
PAPERCUTZ

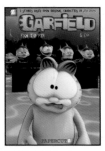

GARFIELD & Co #1
"FISH TO FRY"

GARFIELD
THE CURSE OF THE CAT PEOPLE
& CO.
PAPERCUTZ

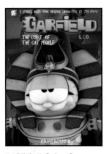

GARFIELD & Co #2
"THE CURSE OF
THE CAT PEOPLE"

GARFIELD
"CATZILLA"
& Co
PAPERCUTZ

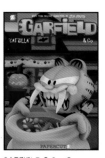

GARFIELD & Co #3
"CATZILLA"

GARFIELD
"CAROLING CAPERS"
& Co
PAPERCUTZ

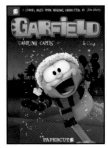

GARFIELD & Co #4
"CAROLING CAPERS"

GARFIELD
A GAME OF CAT AND MOUSE
PAPERCUTZ

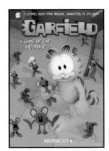

GARFIELD & Co #5
"A GAME OF CAT
AND MOUSE"

GARFIELD
PAPERCUTZ

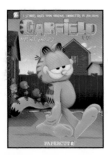

GARFIELD & Co #6
"MOTHER GARFIELD"

GARFIELD
HOME FOR THE HOLIDAYS
PAPERCUTZ

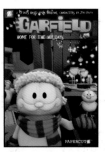

GARFIELD & Co #7
"HOME FOR THE
HOLIDAYS"

GARFIELD
SECRET AGENT X
PAPERCUTZ

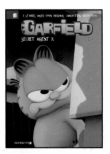

GARFIELD & Co #8
"SECRET AGENT X"

the GARFIELD show
UNFAIR WEATHER
PAPERCUTZ

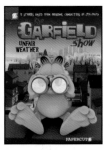

THE GARFIELD SHOW #1
"UNFAIR WEATHER"

the GARFIELD show
JON'S NIGHT OUT
PAPERCUTZ

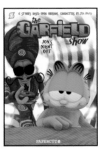

THE GARFIELD SHOW #2
"JON'S NIGHT OUT"

the GARFIELD show
LONG LOST LYMAN
PAPERCUTZ

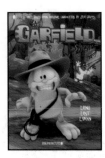

THE GARFIELD SHOW #3
"LONG LOST LYMAN"

the GARFIELD show
LITTLE TROUBLE IN BIG CHINA
PAPERCUTZ

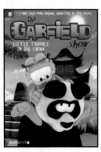

THE GARFIELD SHOW #4
"LITTLE TROUBLE IN
BIG CHINA"

the GARFIELD show
FIDO FOOD FELINE
PAPERCUTZ

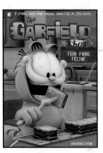

COMING SOON:
THE GARFIELD SHOW #5
"FIDO FOOD FELINE"

GARFIELD & Co GRAPHIC NOVELS ARE AVAILABLE IN HARDCOVER ONLY FOR $7.99 EACH.
THE GARFIELD SHOW GRAPHIC NOVELS ARE $7.99 IN PAPERBACK, AND $11.99 IN HARDCOVER EXCEPT #4 & #5, $12.99 HARDCOVER. AVAILABLE FROM BOOKSELLERS EVERYWHERE.

YOU CAN ALSO ORDER ONLINE FROM PAPERCUTZ.COM OR CALL 1-800-886-1223, MONDAY THROUGH FRIDAY, 9 - 5 EST. MC, VISA, AND AMEX ACCEPTED. TO ORDER BY MAIL, PLEASE ADD $4.00 FOR POSTAGE AND HANDLING FOR FIRST BOOK ORDERED, $1.00 FOR EACH ADDITIONAL BOOK, AND MAKE CHECK PAYABLE TO NBM PUBLISHING. SEND TO: PAPERCUTZ, 160 BROADWAY, SUITE 700, EAST WING, NEW YORK, NY 10038.

GARFIELD & Co AND THE GARFIELD SHOW GRAPHIC NOVELS ARE ALSO AVAILABLE WHEREVER E-BOOKS ARE SOLD.

#4 "LITTLE TROUBLE IN BIG CHINA"

BASED ON THE ORIGINAL CHARACTERS CREATED BY

JIM DAVIS

PAPERCUTZ

NEW YORK

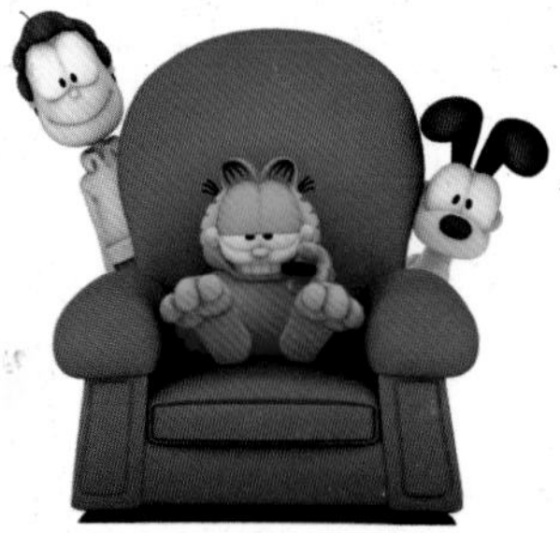

THE GARFIELD SHOW #4 "LITTLE TROUBLE IN BIG CHINA"

 THE GARFIELD SHOW—A DARGAUD MEDIA PRODUCTION. IN ASSOCIATION WITH FRANCE3 WITH THE PARTICIPATION OF CENTRE NATIONAL DE LA CINÉMATOGRAPHIE AND THE SUPPORT OF REGION ILE-DE-FRANCE. A SERIES DEVELOPED BY PHILIPPE VIDAL, ROBERT REA AND STEVE BALISSAT. BASED UPON THE CHARACTERS CREATED BY JIM DAVIS. ORIGINAL STORIES: "LITTLE TROUBLE IN BIG CHINA" WRITTEN BY JULIEN MAGNAT; "FAME FATALE" AND "BORIS THE SNOWMAN" WRITTEN BY PETER BERTS; "MY FRIEND, NERMAL" WRITTEN BY MARK EVANIER.

CEDRIC MICHIELS - COMICS ADAPTATION
JOE JOHNSON - TRANSLATIONS
TONY ISABELLA - DIALOGUE RESTORATION
JANICE CHIANG - LETTERING
ALEXANDER LU - EDITORIAL INTERN
BETH SCORZATO - PRODUCTION COORDINATOR
MICHAEL PETRANEK - EDITOR
JIM SALICRUP
EDITOR-IN-CHIEF

ISBN: 978-1-62991-068-0 PAPERBACK EDITION
ISBN: 978-1-62991-069-7 HARDCOVER EDITION

PRINTED IN CHINA
DECEMBER 2014 BY O.G. PRINTING PRODUCTIONS, LTD.
UNITS 2 & 3, 5/F, LEMMI CENTRE
50 HOI YUEN ROAD
KWON TONG, KOWLOON

PAPERCUTZ BOOKS MAY BE PURCHASED FOR BUSINESS OR PROMOTIONAL USE. FOR INFORMATION ON BULK PURCHASES PLEASE CONTACT MACMILLAN CORPORATE AND PREMIUM SALES DEPARTMENT AT (800) 221-7945 X5442.

DISTRIBUTED BY MACMILLAN
FIRST PAPERCUTZ PRINTING

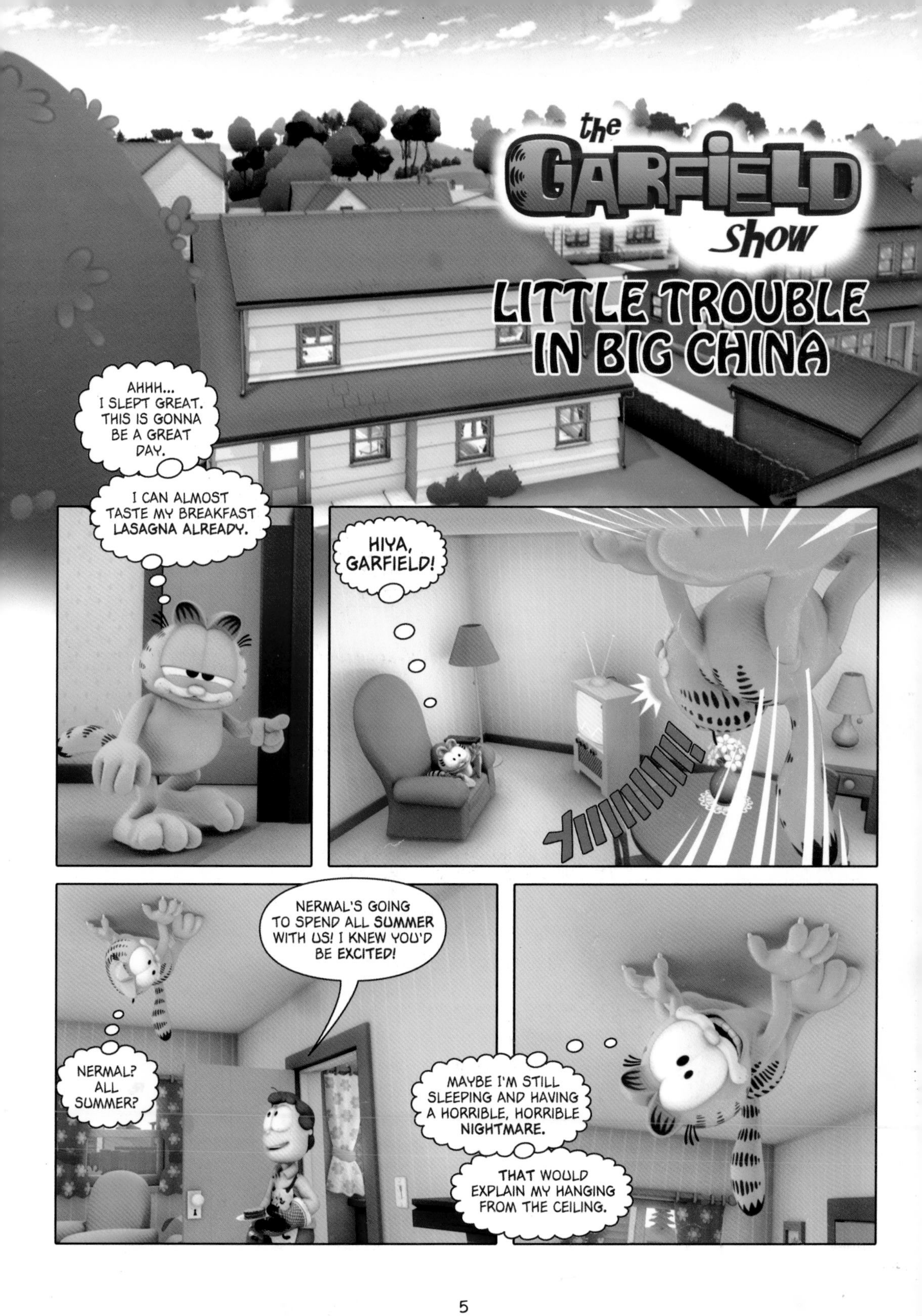
the GARFIELD show
LITTLE TROUBLE IN BIG CHINA
AHHH... I SLEPT GREAT. THIS IS GONNA BE A GREAT DAY.
I CAN ALMOST TASTE MY BREAKFAST LASAGNA ALREADY.
HIYA, GARFIELD!
YIIIIIIIIII!
NERMAL'S GOING TO SPEND ALL SUMMER WITH US! I KNEW YOU'D BE EXCITED!
NERMAL? ALL SUMMER?
MAYBE I'M STILL SLEEPING AND HAVING A HORRIBLE, HORRIBLE NIGHTMARE.
THAT WOULD EXPLAIN MY HANGING FROM THE CEILING.

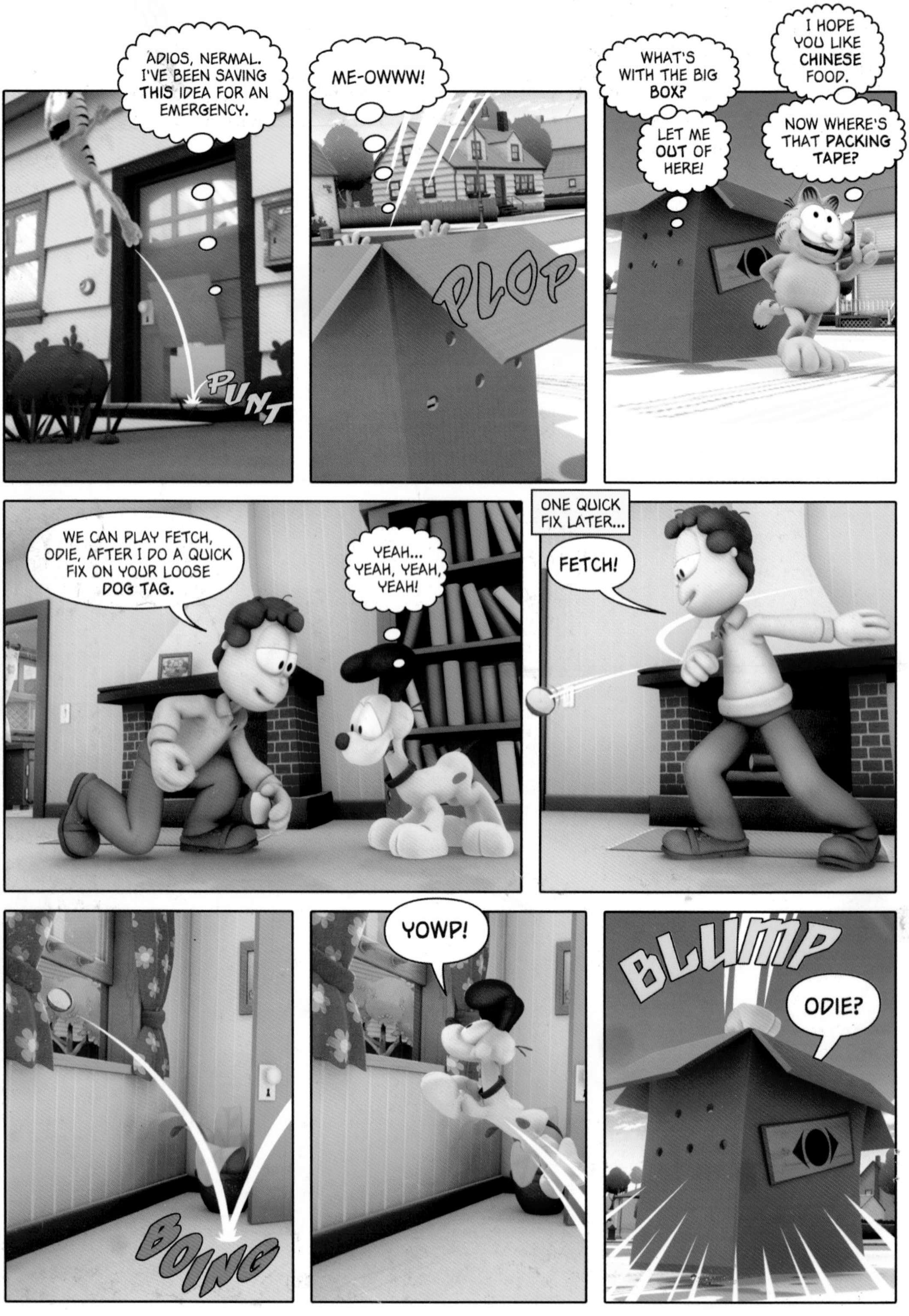

ADIOS, NERMAL. I'VE BEEN SAVING THIS IDEA FOR AN EMERGENCY.
PUNT
ME-OWWW!
PLOP
WHAT'S WITH THE BIG BOX?
I HOPE YOU LIKE CHINESE FOOD.
LET ME OUT OF HERE!
NOW WHERE'S THAT PACKING TAPE?
WE CAN PLAY FETCH, ODIE, AFTER I DO A QUICK FIX ON YOUR LOOSE DOG TAG.
YEAH... YEAH, YEAH, YEAH!
ONE QUICK FIX LATER...
FETCH!
BOING
YOWP!
BLUMP
ODIE?

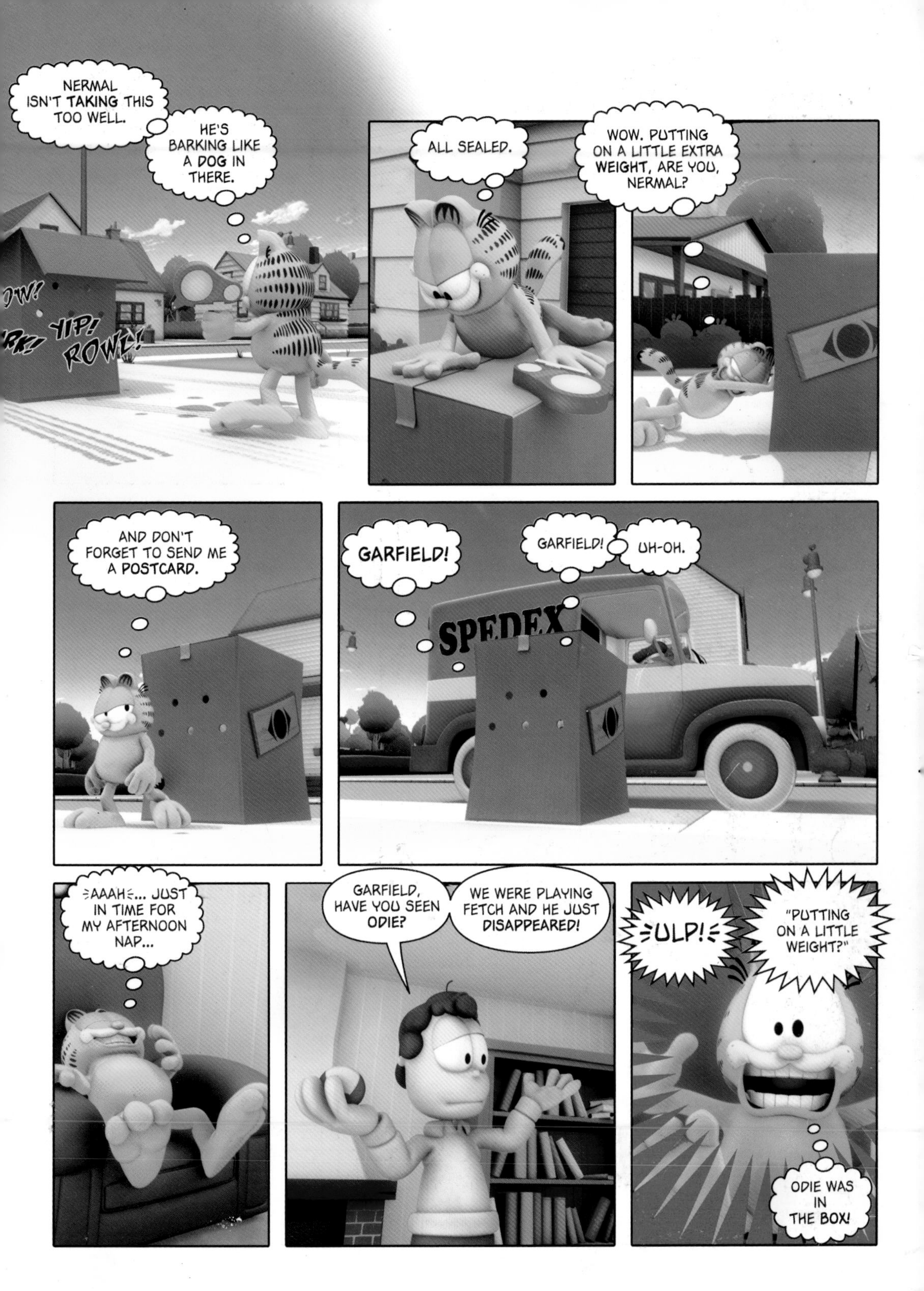
NERMAL ISN'T TAKING THIS TOO WELL.
HE'S BARKING LIKE A DOG IN THERE.
YIP!
ROWL!
ALL SEALED.
WOW. PUTTING ON A LITTLE EXTRA WEIGHT, ARE YOU, NERMAL?
AND DON'T FORGET TO SEND ME A POSTCARD.
GARFIELD!
GARFIELD!
UH-OH.
SPEDEX
AAAH... JUST IN TIME FOR MY AFTERNOON NAP...
GARFIELD, HAVE YOU SEEN ODIE?
WE WERE PLAYING FETCH AND HE JUST DISAPPEARED!
ULP!
"PUTTING ON A LITTLE WEIGHT?"
ODIE WAS IN THE BOX!

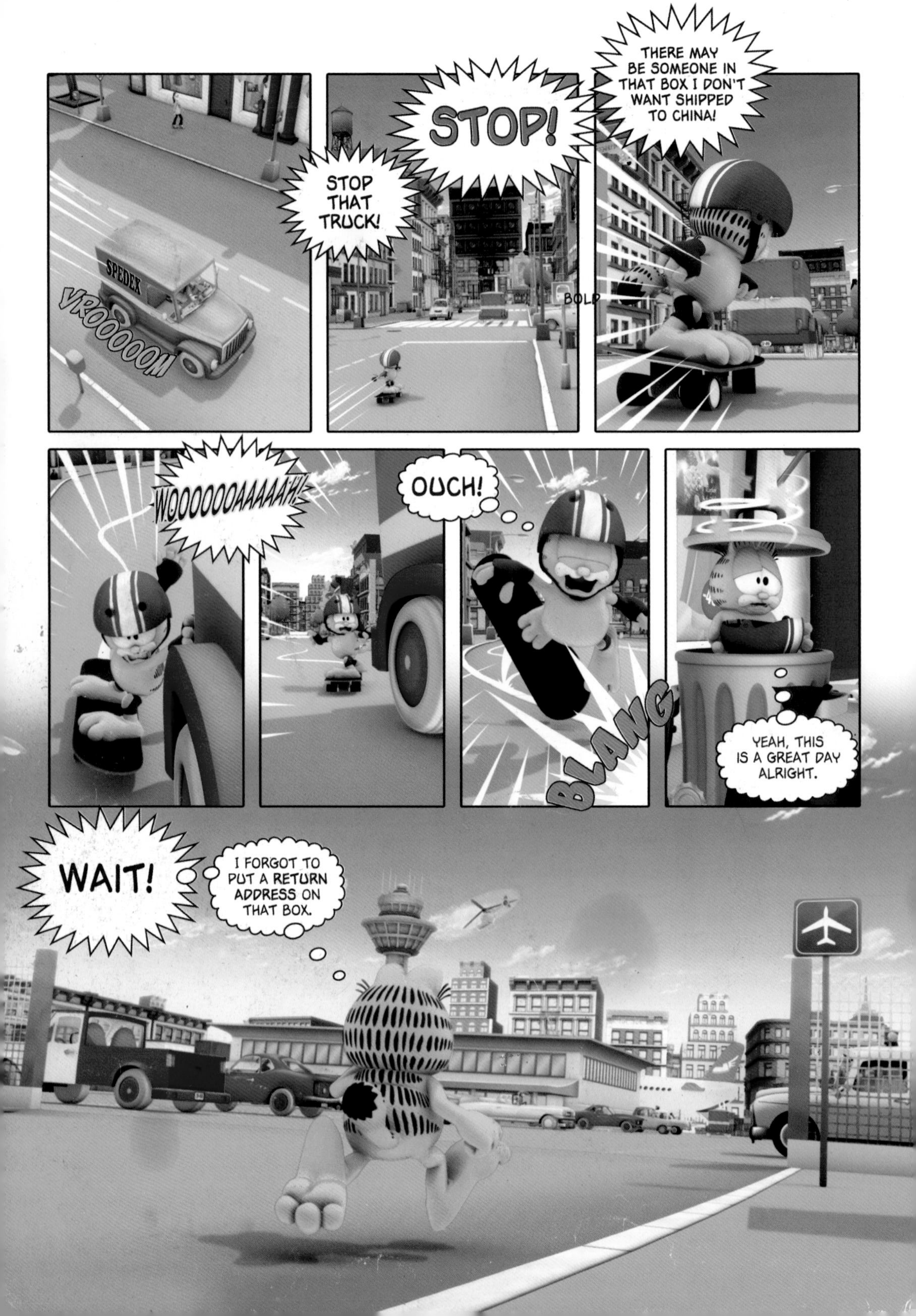

SPEDEX
VROOOOOOM
STOP THAT TRUCK!
STOP!
THERE MAY BE SOMEONE IN THAT BOX I DON'T WANT SHIPPED TO CHINA!
WOOOOOOAAAAAH!
OUCH!
BLANG
YEAH, THIS IS A GREAT DAY ALRIGHT.
WAIT!
I FORGOT TO PUT A RETURN ADDRESS ON THAT BOX.

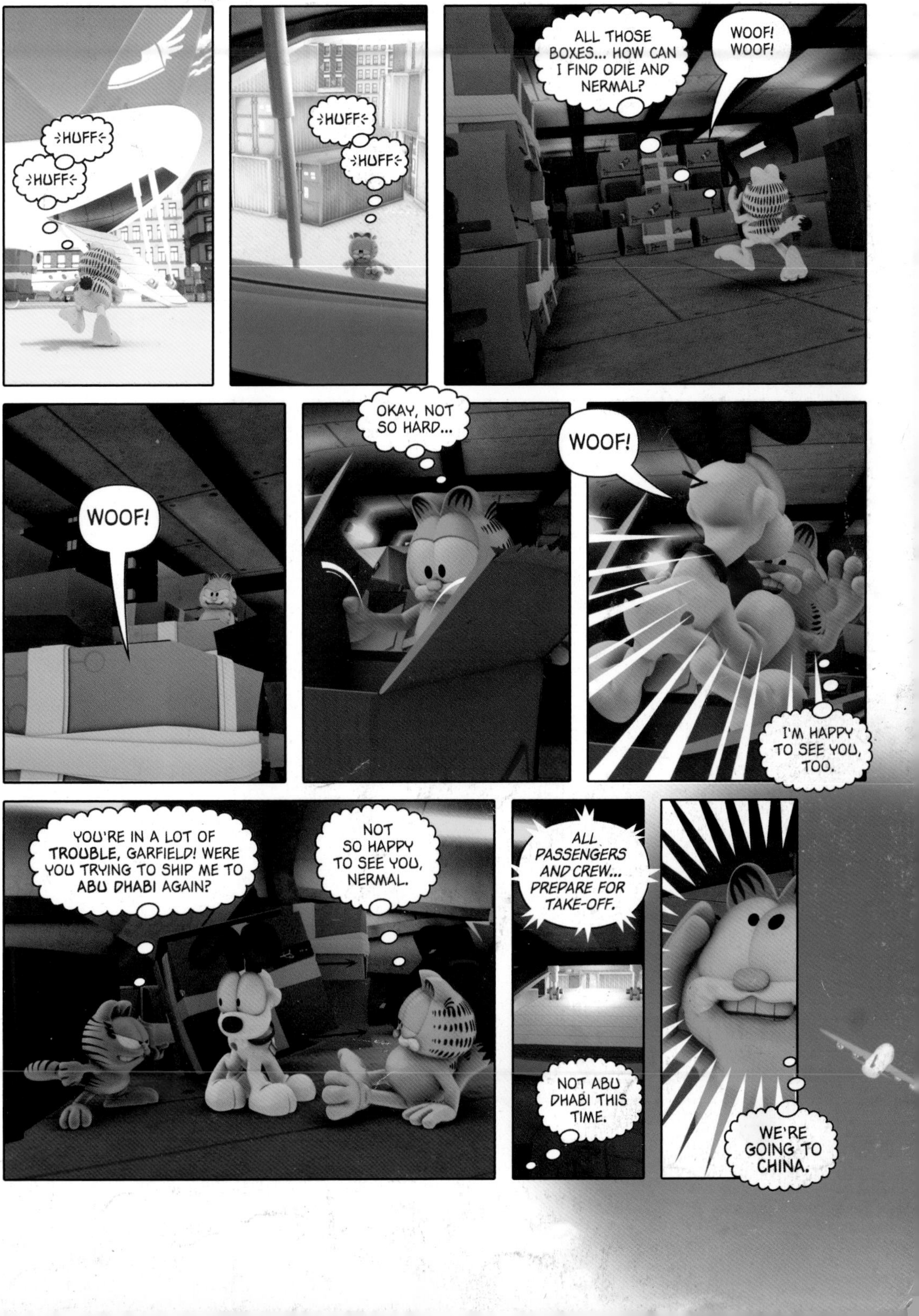

HUFF
HUFF
HUFF
HUFF
ALL THOSE BOXES... HOW CAN I FIND ODIE AND NERMAL?
WOOF! WOOF!
WOOF!
OKAY, NOT SO HARD...
WOOF!
I'M HAPPY TO SEE YOU, TOO.
YOU'RE IN A LOT OF TROUBLE, GARFIELD! WERE YOU TRYING TO SHIP ME TO ABU DHABI AGAIN?
NOT SO HAPPY TO SEE YOU, NERMAL.
ALL PASSENGERS AND CREW... PREPARE FOR TAKE-OFF.
NOT ABU DHABI THIS TIME.
WE'RE GOING TO CHINA.

CHINA...

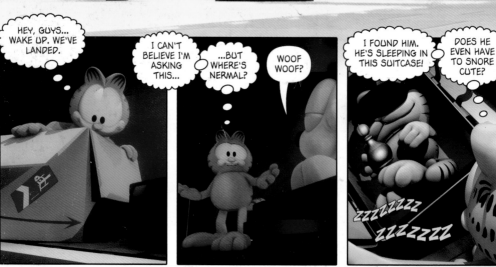

HEY, GUYS... WAKE UP. WE'VE LANDED.

I CAN'T BELIEVE I'M ASKING THIS...

...BUT WHERE'S NERMAL?

WOOF WOOF?

I FOUND HIM. HE'S SLEEPING IN THIS SUITCASE!

DOES HE EVEN HAVE TO SNORE CUTE?

ZZZZZZZ
ZZZZZZZ

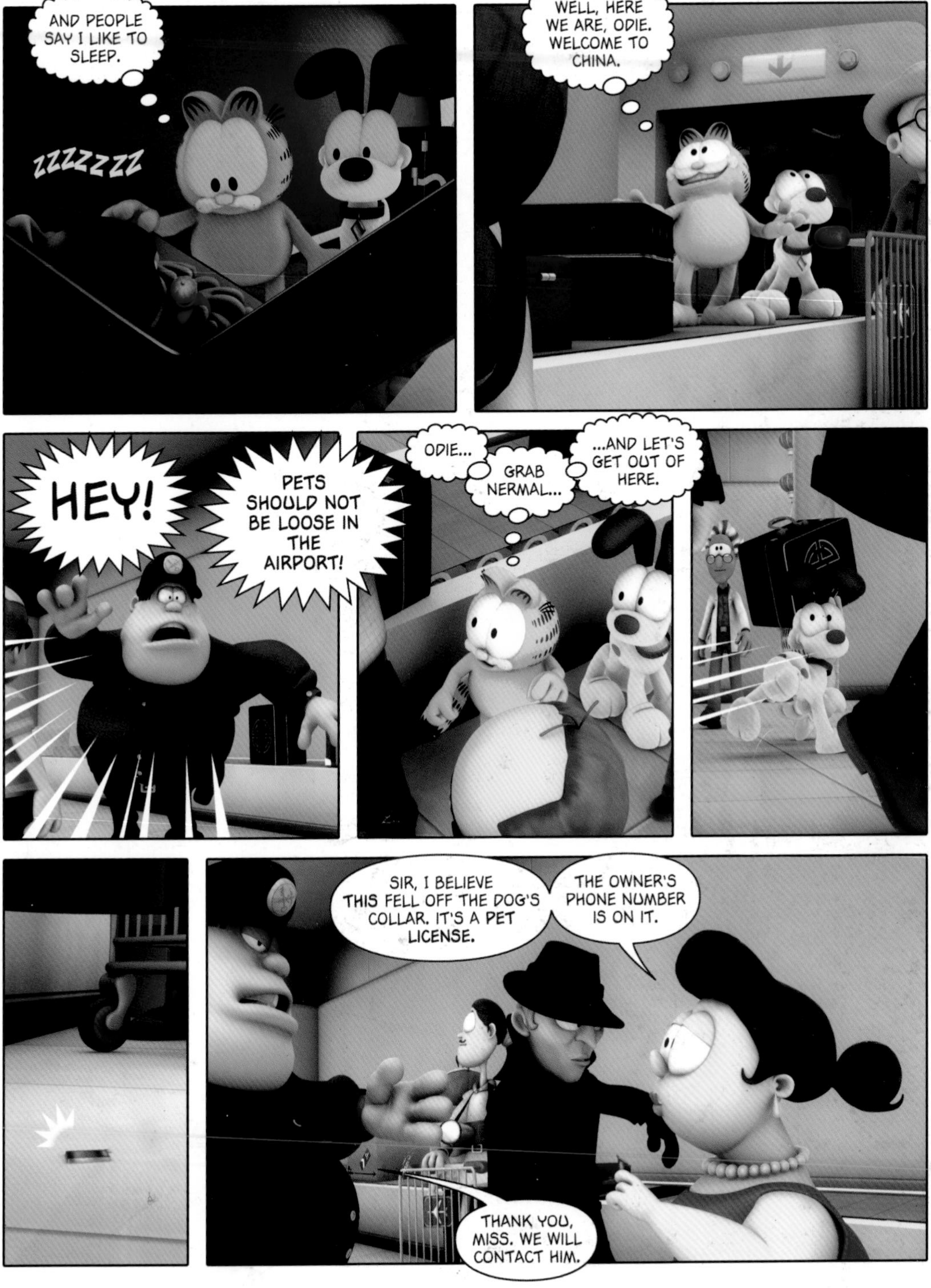
AND PEOPLE SAY I LIKE TO SLEEP.
ZZZZZZZ
WELL, HERE WE ARE, ODIE. WELCOME TO CHINA.
HEY!
PETS SHOULD NOT BE LOOSE IN THE AIRPORT!
ODIE...
GRAB NERMAL...
...AND LET'S GET OUT OF HERE.
SIR, I BELIEVE THIS FELL OFF THE DOG'S COLLAR. IT'S A PET LICENSE.
THE OWNER'S PHONE NUMBER IS ON IT.
THANK YOU, MISS. WE WILL CONTACT HIM.

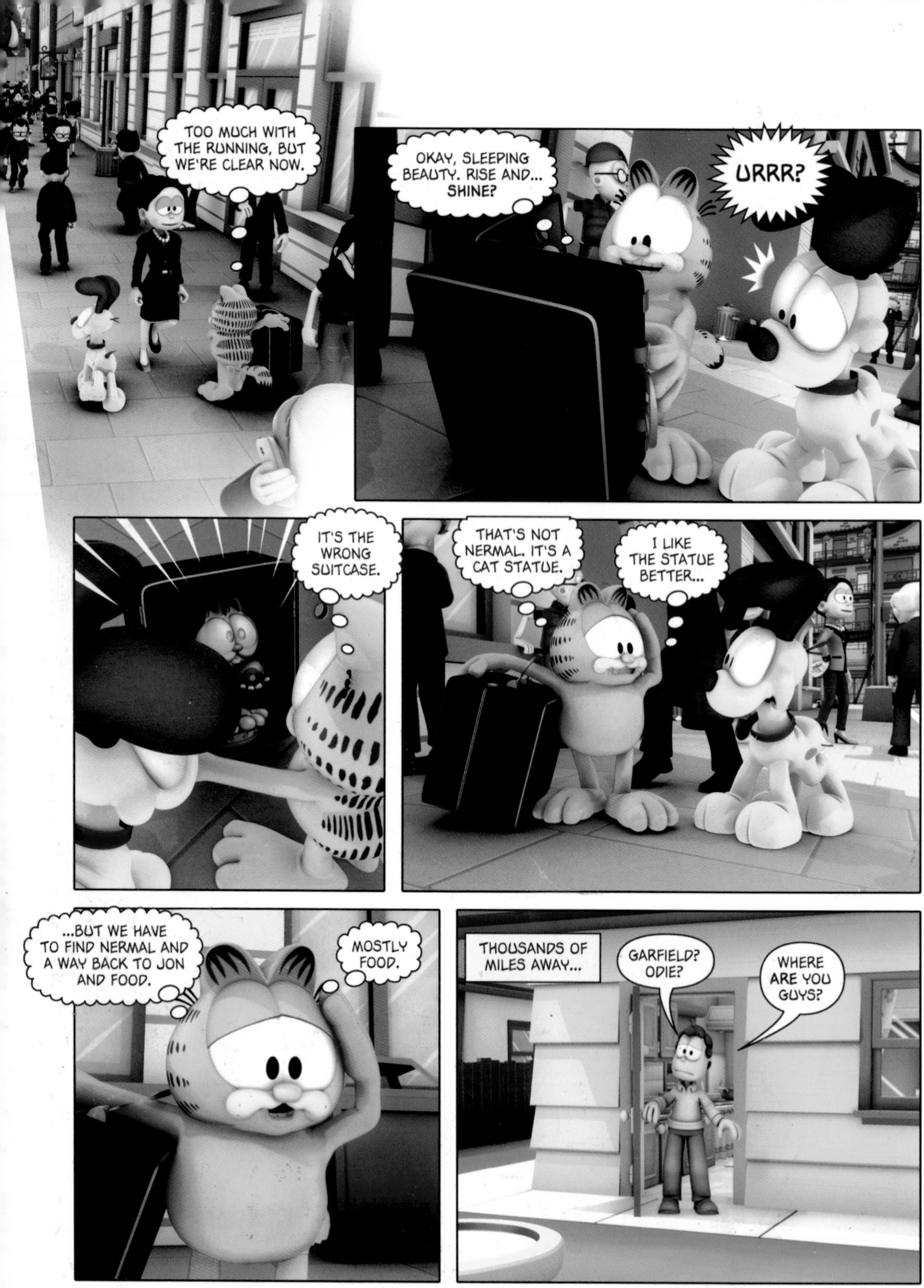
TOO MUCH WITH THE RUNNING, BUT WE'RE CLEAR NOW.
OKAY, SLEEPING BEAUTY. RISE AND... SHINE?
URRR?
IT'S THE WRONG SUITCASE.
THAT'S NOT NERMAL. IT'S A CAT STATUE.
I LIKE THE STATUE BETTER...
...BUT WE HAVE TO FIND NERMAL AND A WAY BACK TO JON AND FOOD.
MOSTLY FOOD.
THOUSANDS OF MILES AWAY...
GARFIELD? ODIE?
WHERE ARE YOU GUYS?

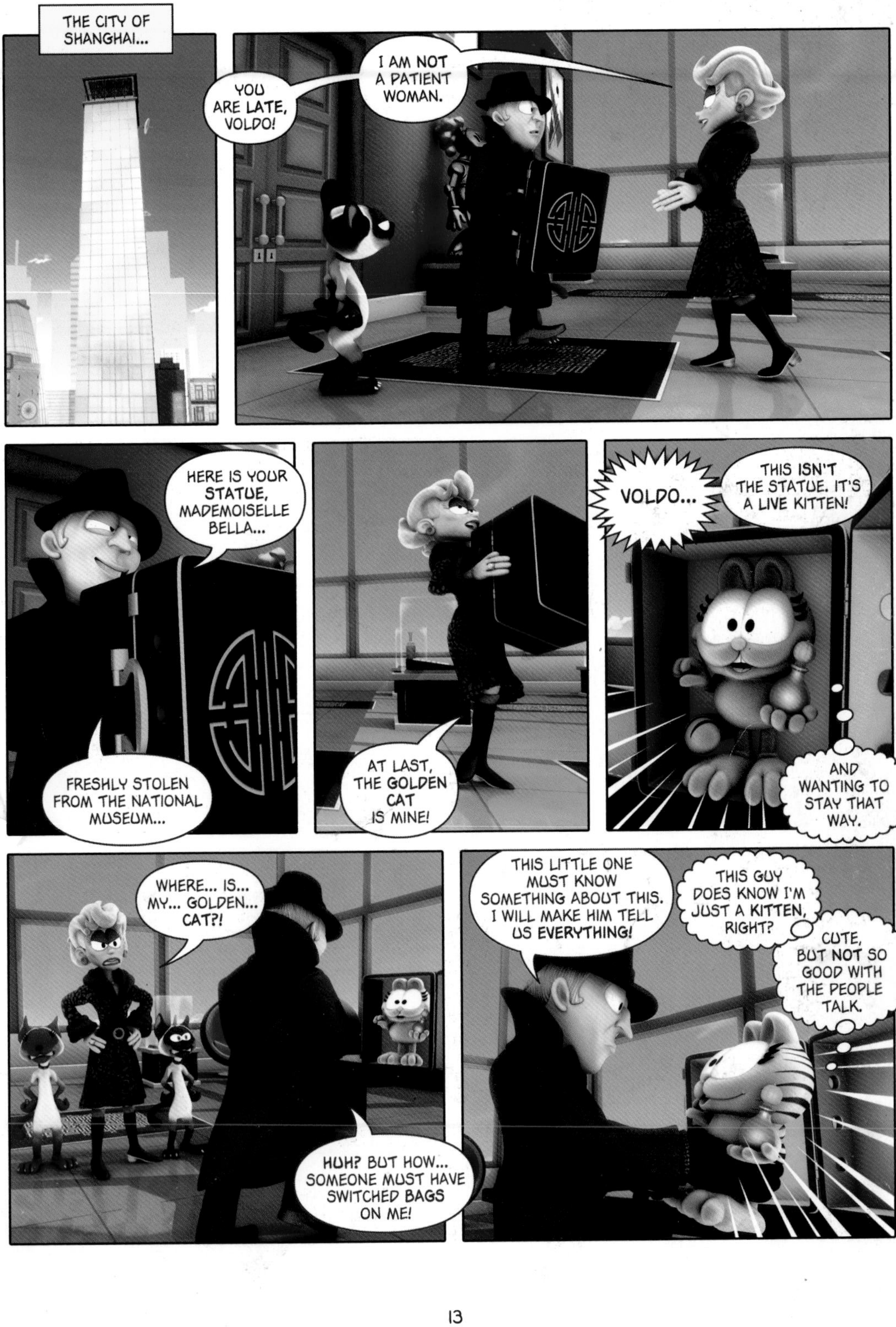
THE CITY OF SHANGHAI...
YOU ARE LATE, VOLDO!
I AM NOT A PATIENT WOMAN.
HERE IS YOUR STATUE, MADEMOISELLE BELLA...
FRESHLY STOLEN FROM THE NATIONAL MUSEUM...
AT LAST, THE GOLDEN CAT IS MINE!
VOLDO...
THIS ISN'T THE STATUE. IT'S A LIVE KITTEN!
AND WANTING TO STAY THAT WAY.
WHERE... IS... MY... GOLDEN... CAT?!
HUH? BUT HOW... SOMEONE MUST HAVE SWITCHED BAGS ON ME!
THIS LITTLE ONE MUST KNOW SOMETHING ABOUT THIS. I WILL MAKE HIM TELL US EVERYTHING!
THIS GUY DOES KNOW I'M JUST A KITTEN, RIGHT?
CUTE, BUT NOT SO GOOD WITH THE PEOPLE TALK.

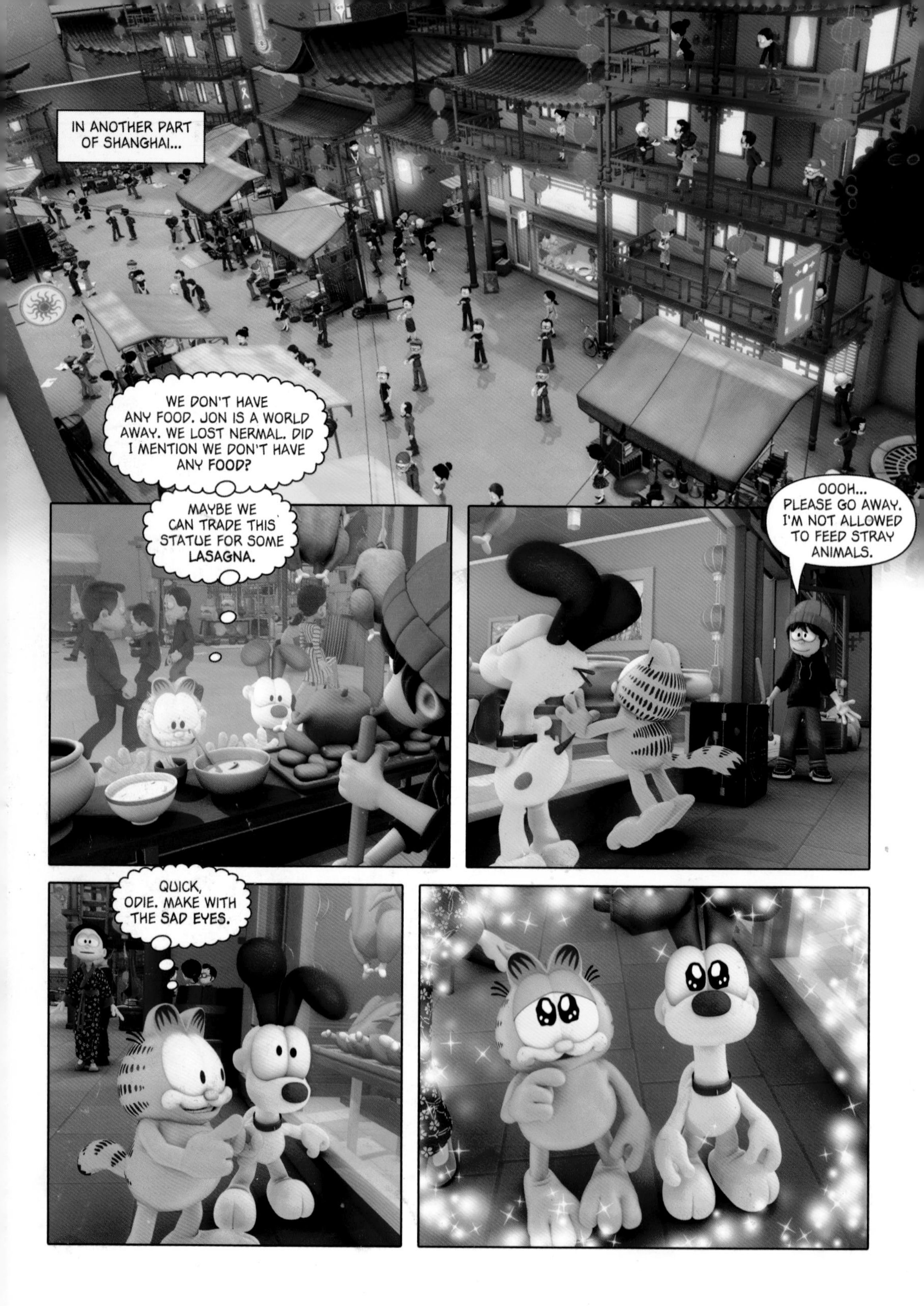
IN ANOTHER PART OF SHANGHAI...
WE DON'T HAVE ANY FOOD. JON IS A WORLD AWAY. WE LOST NERMAL. DID I MENTION WE DON'T HAVE ANY FOOD?
MAYBE WE CAN TRADE THIS STATUE FOR SOME LASAGNA.
OOOH... PLEASE GO AWAY. I'M NOT ALLOWED TO FEED STRAY ANIMALS.
QUICK, ODIE. MAKE WITH THE SAD EYES.

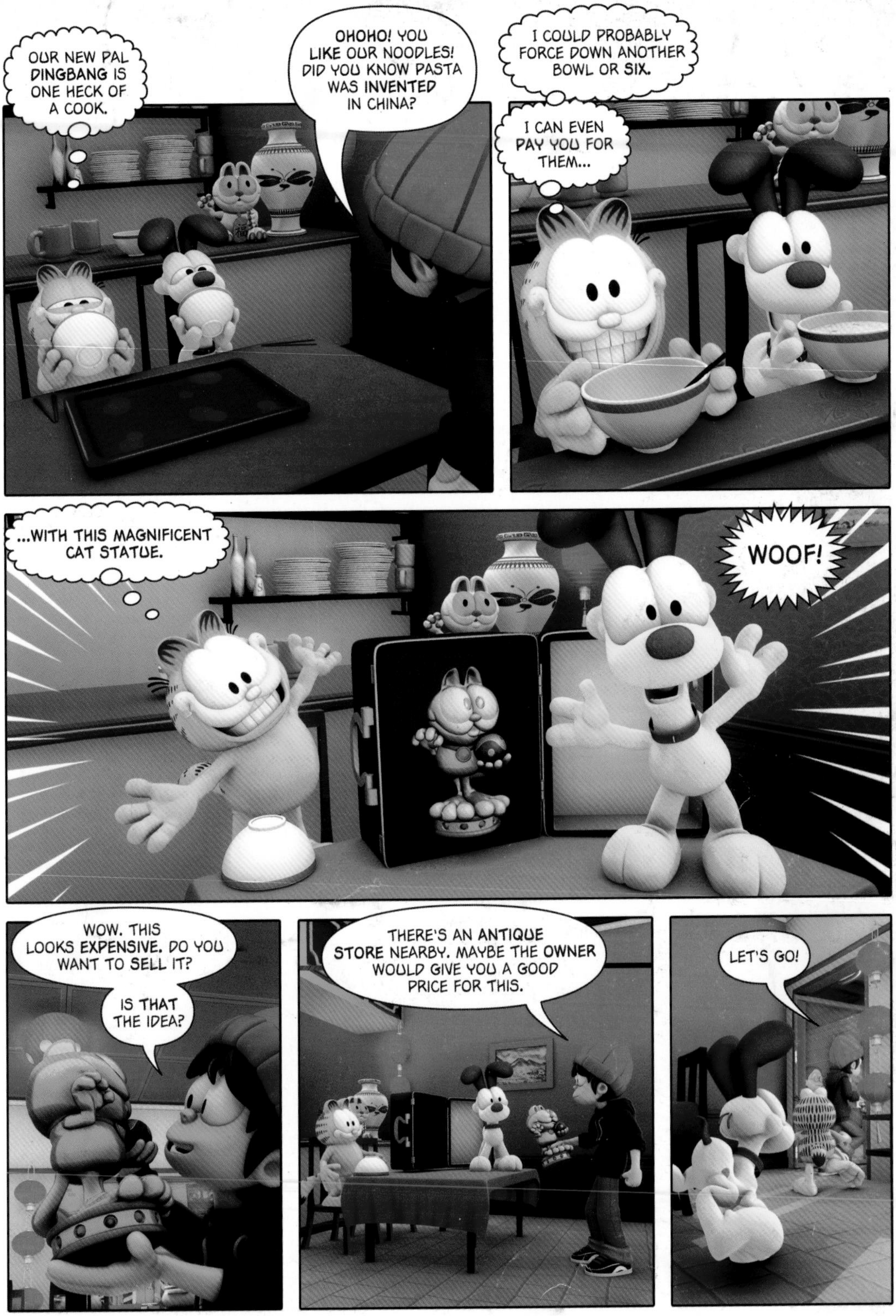
OUR NEW PAL DINGBANG IS ONE HECK OF A COOK.
OHOHO! YOU LIKE OUR NOODLES! DID YOU KNOW PASTA WAS INVENTED IN CHINA?
I COULD PROBABLY FORCE DOWN ANOTHER BOWL OR SIX.
I CAN EVEN PAY YOU FOR THEM...
...WITH THIS MAGNIFICENT CAT STATUE.
WOOF!
WOW. THIS LOOKS EXPENSIVE. DO YOU WANT TO SELL IT?
IS THAT THE IDEA?
THERE'S AN ANTIQUE STORE NEARBY. MAYBE THE OWNER WOULD GIVE YOU A GOOD PRICE FOR THIS.
LET'S GO!

AN OCEAN AWAY...

SORRY, JON. I HAVEN'T SEEN GARFIELD, ODIE, OR THAT CUTE ONE.

HELLO?

RINGA RINGA

MY DOG AND A CAT? YOU'VE SEEN THEM?

WHERE DID YOU SEE THEM?

IN CH-CH-- CHINA?!

WELCOME TO OUR NON-STOP FLIGHT TO SHANGHAI.

HERMAN SAID THE BOX WAS MAILED TO SHANGHAI, BUT HOW WILL I FIND THEM?

THAT CITY IS HUGE!

A CAT AND A DOG CREATED HAVOC IN SHANGHAI AIRPORT...

...AND RAN OFF WITH THE LUGGAGE OF BELLA BELLISSIMA.

THE WEALTHY HEIRESS IS OFFERING A LARGE REWARD...

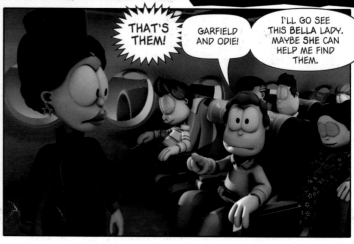

THAT'S THEM!

GARFIELD AND ODIE!

I'LL GO SEE THIS BELLA LADY. MAYBE SHE CAN HELP ME FIND THEM.

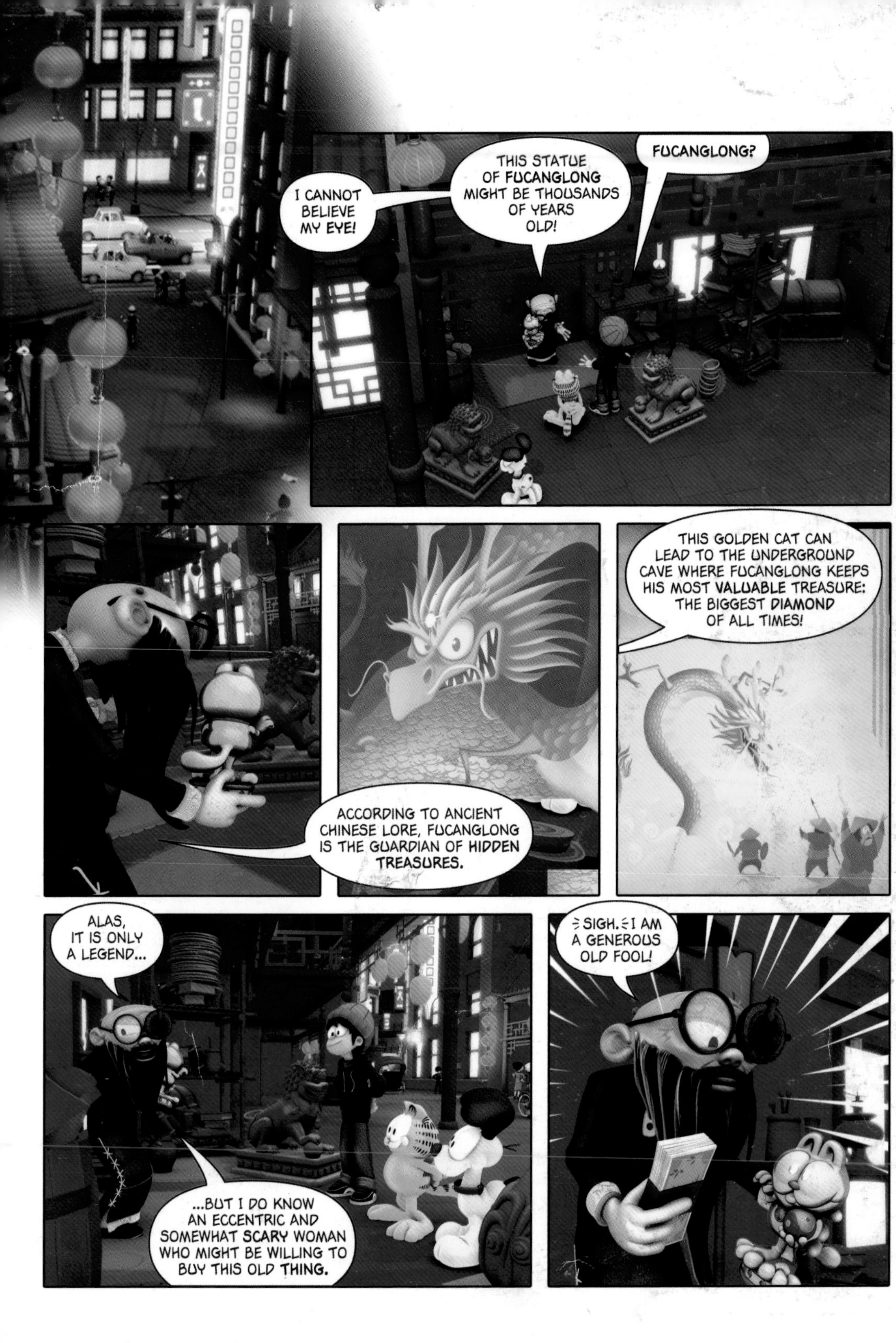
I CANNOT BELIEVE MY EYE!
THIS STATUE OF FUCANGLONG MIGHT BE THOUSANDS OF YEARS OLD!
FUCANGLONG?
ACCORDING TO ANCIENT CHINESE LORE, FUCANGLONG IS THE GUARDIAN OF HIDDEN TREASURES.
THIS GOLDEN CAT CAN LEAD TO THE UNDERGROUND CAVE WHERE FUCANGLONG KEEPS HIS MOST VALUABLE TREASURE: THE BIGGEST DIAMOND OF ALL TIMES!
ALAS, IT IS ONLY A LEGEND...
...BUT I DO KNOW AN ECCENTRIC AND SOMEWHAT SCARY WOMAN WHO MIGHT BE WILLING TO BUY THIS OLD THING.
SIGH. I AM A GENEROUS OLD FOOL!

TEN THOUSAND? THAT SOUNDS LIKE A LOT OF NOODLE MONEY TO ME.

SORRY, BUT IT IS NOT FOR SALE.

COME, MY FRIENDS.

HUH?

I'LL HAVE TO SETTLE FOR A FINDER'S FEE.

MISS BELLA, I KNOW WHO HAS YOUR GOLDEN CAT.

BUT THAT INFORMATION WILL COST YOU.

SPEAK, MERCHANT! YOU SHALL HAVE YOUR MONEY.

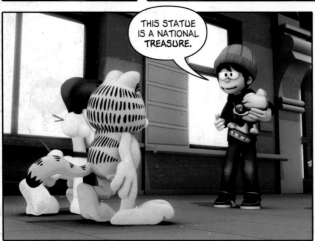

THIS STATUE IS A NATIONAL TREASURE.

IT BELONGS IN A CHINESE MUSEUM WHERE MY PEOPLE CAN ENJOY IT...

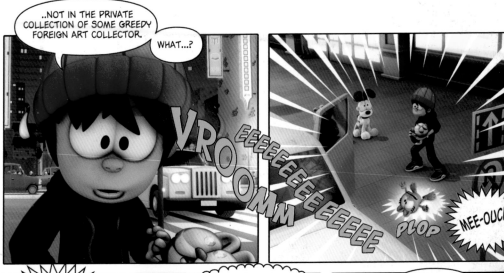

..NOT IN THE PRIVATE COLLECTION OF SOME GREEDY FOREIGN ART COLLECTOR.

WHAT...?

VROOMM EEEEEEEEEEEEEE

PLOP

MEE-OUCH!

NERMAL!

GARFIELD!

YOU ABANDONED ME! SOME GOON WORKING FOR A WACKY WOMAN KIDNAPPED ME! THEY'RE LOOKING FOR SOME OLD STATUE!

THEY'RE CRAZY HERE! I WANT TO GO HOME!

WE SHOULD GO BACK TO THE RESTAURANT.

IS THIS CUTE LITTLE KITTEN A FRIEND OF YOURS?

DOES "FRIEND" MEAN "LOATHSOMELY CUTE" OVER HERE?

I'M NOT FEELING THE LOVE, GARFIELD.

IT'S LIKE YOU'RE NOT HAPPY TO SEE ME!

IT'S JUST LUCKY SHE DUMPED ME ON THE STREET IN FRONT OF YOU!

DOES "LUCKY" MEAN... OH, NEVER MIND.

19

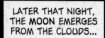
LATER THAT NIGHT, THE MOON EMERGES FROM THE CLOUDS...

...AND ITS LIGHT WASHES OVER THE GOLDEN CAT.

LOOK!

THE MOONBEAM IS REFLECTED IN THE STATUE'S EYES.

THERE'S ALSO WRITING: "THE FIRST HALF OF THE KEY TO FUCANGLONG'S TREASURE IS HIDDEN IN THE ANCIENT GARDENS OF SUJO."

IT'S PROJECTING AN IMAGE OF A TIGER HEAD! WHAT DOES THAT MEAN?

SUJO IS CLOSE. WE'LL SEARCH FOR THE KEY TOMORROW.

WOO! TREASURE MAP.

THAT'S KINDA EXCITING.

BUT BELLA'S CATS...

HSSSSSS HSSS

...HAVE BEEN LISTENING.

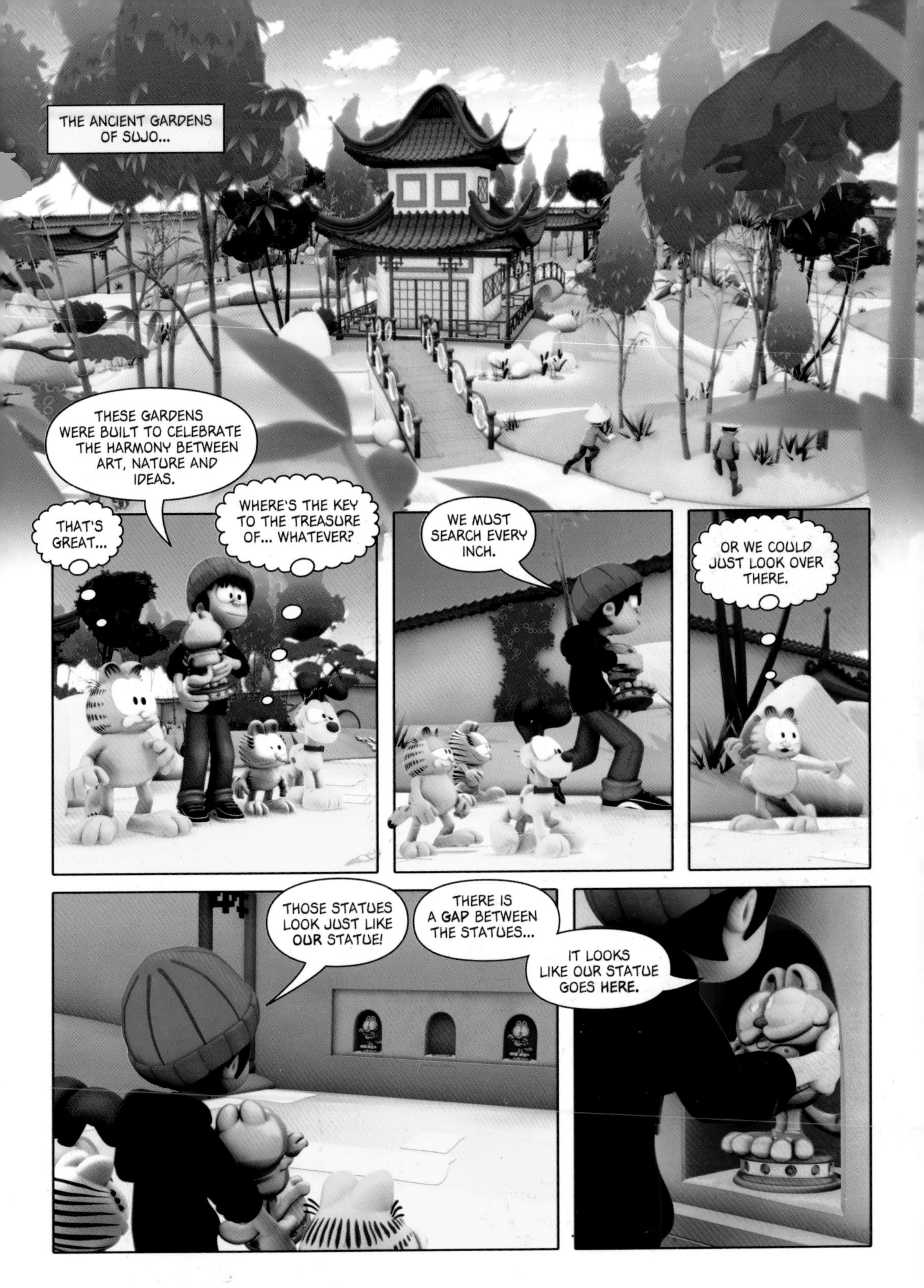
THE ANCIENT GARDENS OF SUJO...
THESE GARDENS WERE BUILT TO CELEBRATE THE HARMONY BETWEEN ART, NATURE AND IDEAS.
THAT'S GREAT...
WHERE'S THE KEY TO THE TREASURE OF... WHATEVER?
WE MUST SEARCH EVERY INCH.
OR WE COULD JUST LOOK OVER THERE.
THOSE STATUES LOOK JUST LIKE OUR STATUE!
THERE IS A GAP BETWEEN THE STATUES...
IT LOOKS LIKE OUR STATUE GOES HERE.

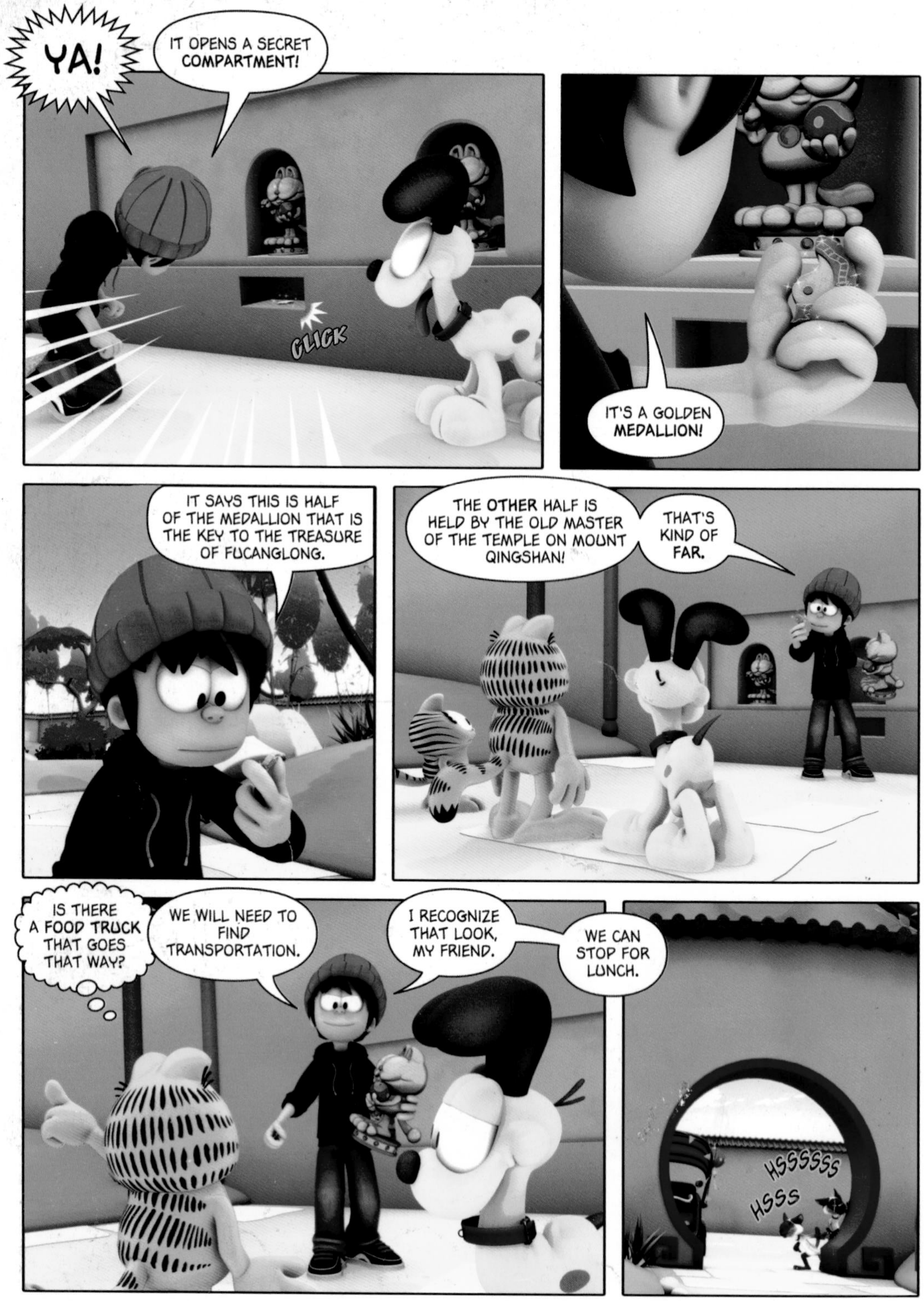
YA!
IT OPENS A SECRET COMPARTMENT!
CLICK
IT'S A GOLDEN MEDALLION!
IT SAYS THIS IS HALF OF THE MEDALLION THAT IS THE KEY TO THE TREASURE OF FUCANGLONG.
THE OTHER HALF IS HELD BY THE OLD MASTER OF THE TEMPLE ON MOUNT QINGSHAN!
THAT'S KIND OF FAR.
IS THERE A FOOD TRUCK THAT GOES THAT WAY?
WE WILL NEED TO FIND TRANSPORTATION.
I RECOGNIZE THAT LOOK, MY FRIEND.
WE CAN STOP FOR LUNCH.
HSSSSSS
HSSS

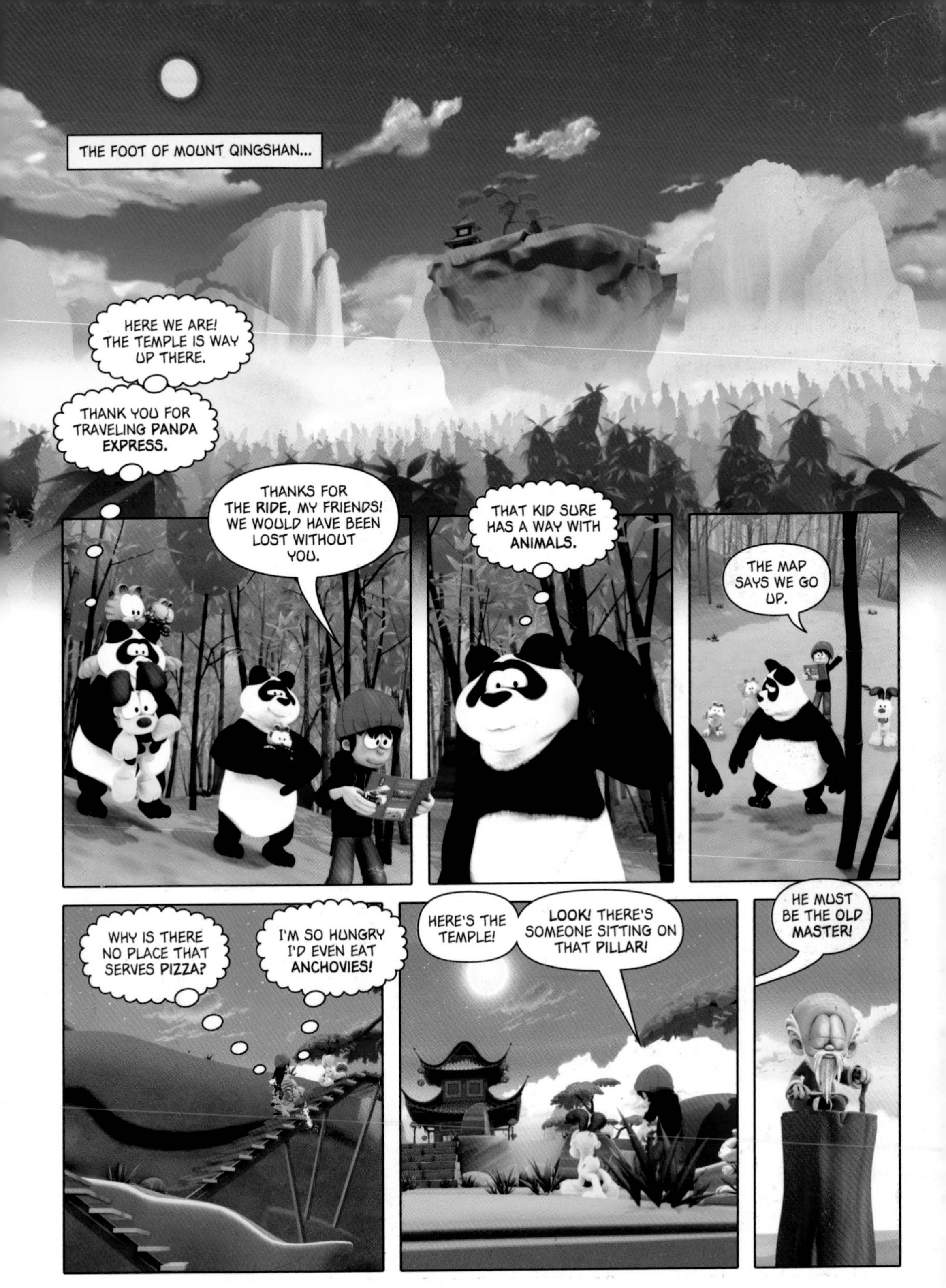
THE FOOT OF MOUNT QINGSHAN...
HERE WE ARE! THE TEMPLE IS WAY UP THERE.
THANK YOU FOR TRAVELING PANDA EXPRESS.
THANKS FOR THE RIDE, MY FRIENDS! WE WOULD HAVE BEEN LOST WITHOUT YOU.
THAT KID SURE HAS A WAY WITH ANIMALS.
THE MAP SAYS WE GO UP.
WHY IS THERE NO PLACE THAT SERVES PIZZA?
I'M SO HUNGRY I'D EVEN EAT ANCHOVIES!
HERE'S THE TEMPLE!
LOOK! THERE'S SOMEONE SITTING ON THAT PILLAR!
HE MUST BE THE OLD MASTER!

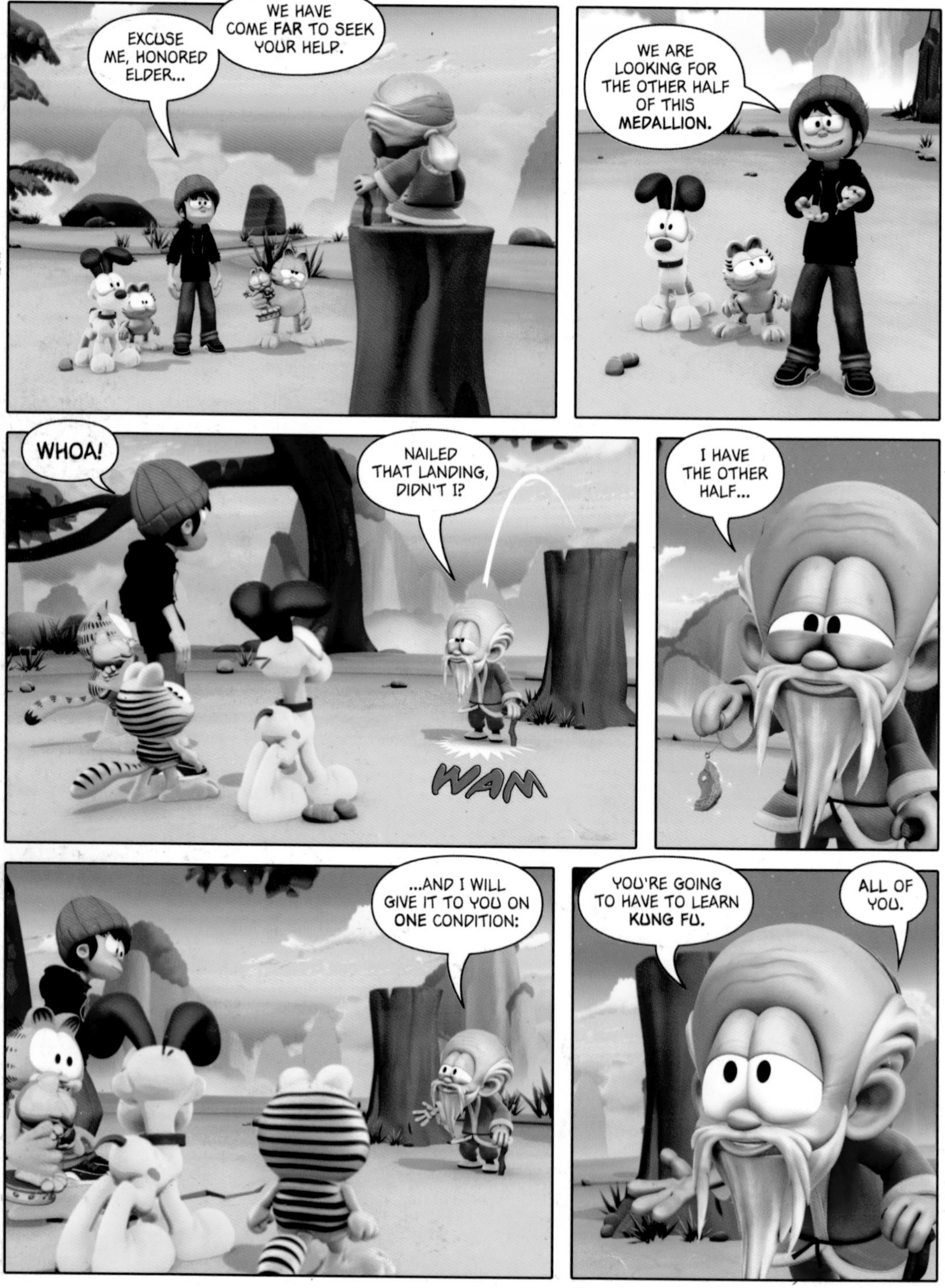
EXCUSE ME, HONORED ELDER...
WE HAVE COME FAR TO SEEK YOUR HELP.
WE ARE LOOKING FOR THE OTHER HALF OF THIS MEDALLION.
WHOA!
NAILED THAT LANDING, DIDN'T I?
WAM
I HAVE THE OTHER HALF...
...AND I WILL GIVE IT TO YOU ON ONE CONDITION:
YOU'RE GOING TO HAVE TO LEARN KUNG FU.
ALL OF YOU.

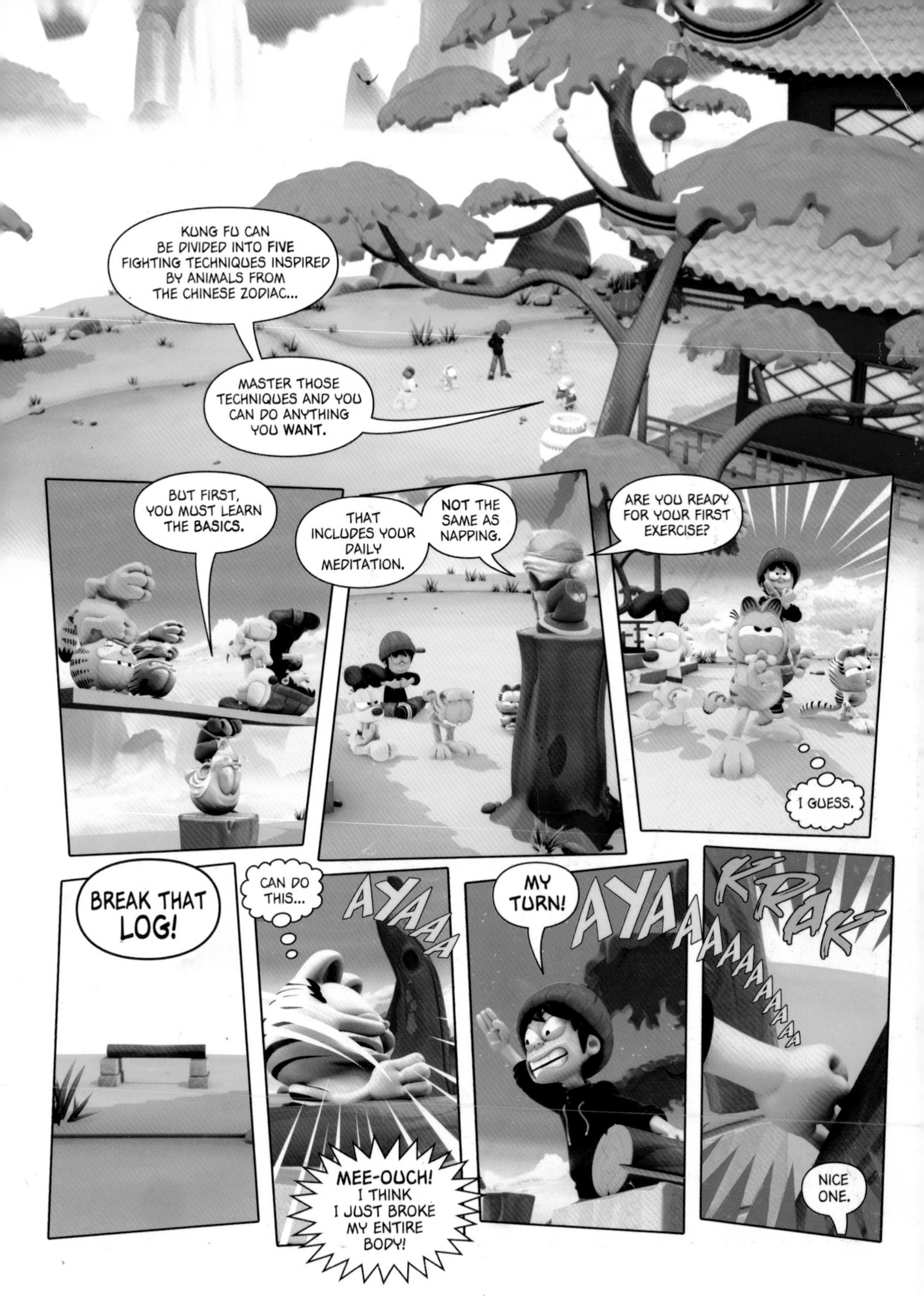
KUNG FU CAN BE DIVIDED INTO FIVE FIGHTING TECHNIQUES INSPIRED BY ANIMALS FROM THE CHINESE ZODIAC...
MASTER THOSE TECHNIQUES AND YOU CAN DO ANYTHING YOU WANT.
BUT FIRST, YOU MUST LEARN THE BASICS.
THAT INCLUDES YOUR DAILY MEDITATION.
NOT THE SAME AS NAPPING.
ARE YOU READY FOR YOUR FIRST EXERCISE?
I GUESS.
BREAK THAT LOG!
CAN DO THIS...
AYAAA
MEE-OUCH! I THINK I JUST BROKE MY ENTIRE BODY!
MY TURN!
AYAAAAAAAAAAAAA
KRAK
NICE ONE.

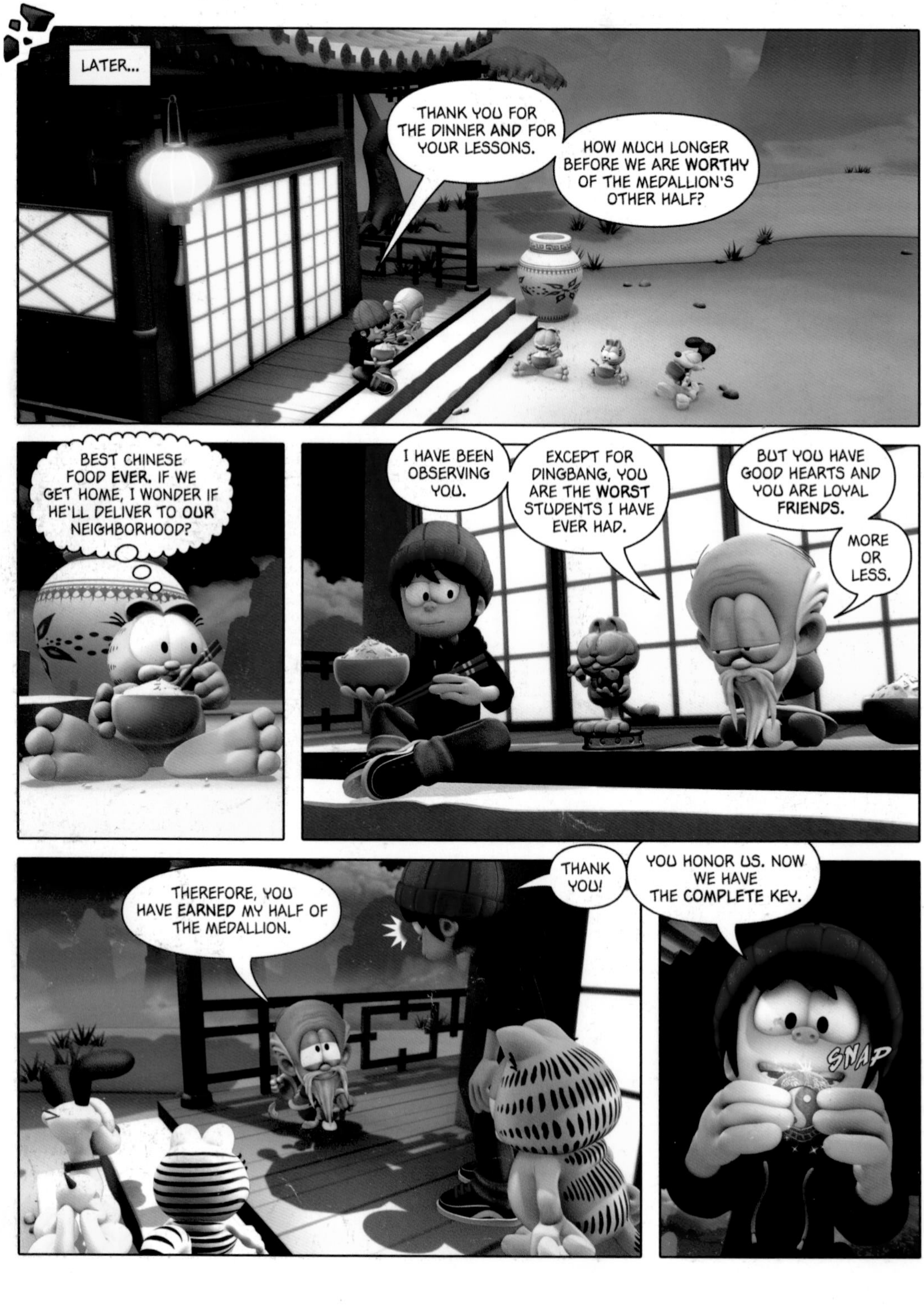
LATER...
THANK YOU FOR THE DINNER AND FOR YOUR LESSONS.
HOW MUCH LONGER BEFORE WE ARE WORTHY OF THE MEDALLION'S OTHER HALF?
BEST CHINESE FOOD EVER. IF WE GET HOME, I WONDER IF HE'LL DELIVER TO OUR NEIGHBORHOOD?
I HAVE BEEN OBSERVING YOU.
EXCEPT FOR DINGBANG, YOU ARE THE WORST STUDENTS I HAVE EVER HAD.
BUT YOU HAVE GOOD HEARTS AND YOU ARE LOYAL FRIENDS.
MORE OR LESS.
THEREFORE, YOU HAVE EARNED MY HALF OF THE MEDALLION.
THANK YOU!
YOU HONOR US. NOW WE HAVE THE COMPLETE KEY.
SNAP

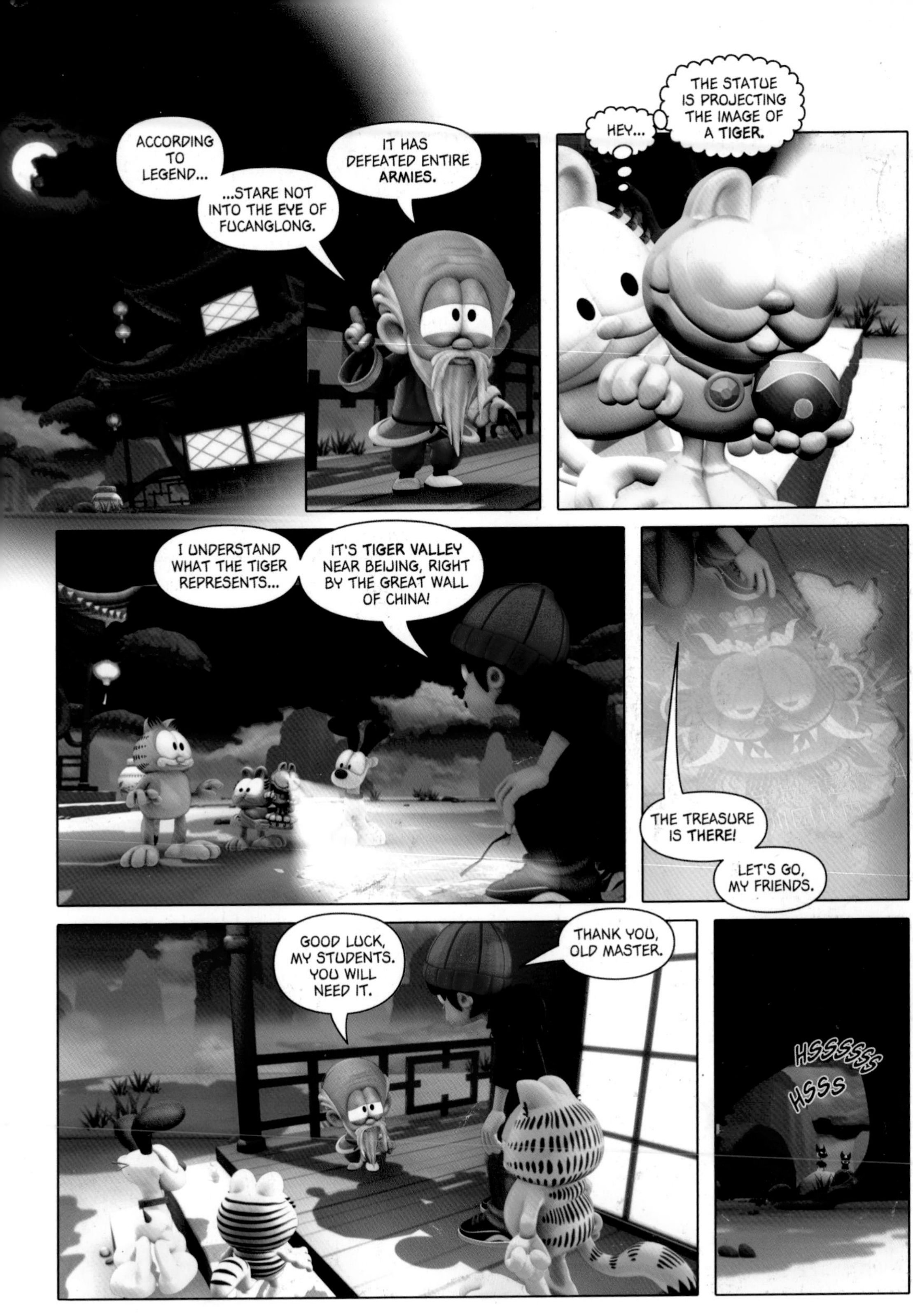

ACCORDING TO LEGEND...
...STARE NOT INTO THE EYE OF FUCANGLONG.
IT HAS DEFEATED ENTIRE ARMIES.
HEY...
THE STATUE IS PROJECTING THE IMAGE OF A TIGER.
I UNDERSTAND WHAT THE TIGER REPRESENTS...
IT'S TIGER VALLEY NEAR BEIJING, RIGHT BY THE GREAT WALL OF CHINA!
THE TREASURE IS THERE!
LET'S GO, MY FRIENDS.
GOOD LUCK, MY STUDENTS. YOU WILL NEED IT.
THANK YOU, OLD MASTER.
HSSSSSS
HSSS

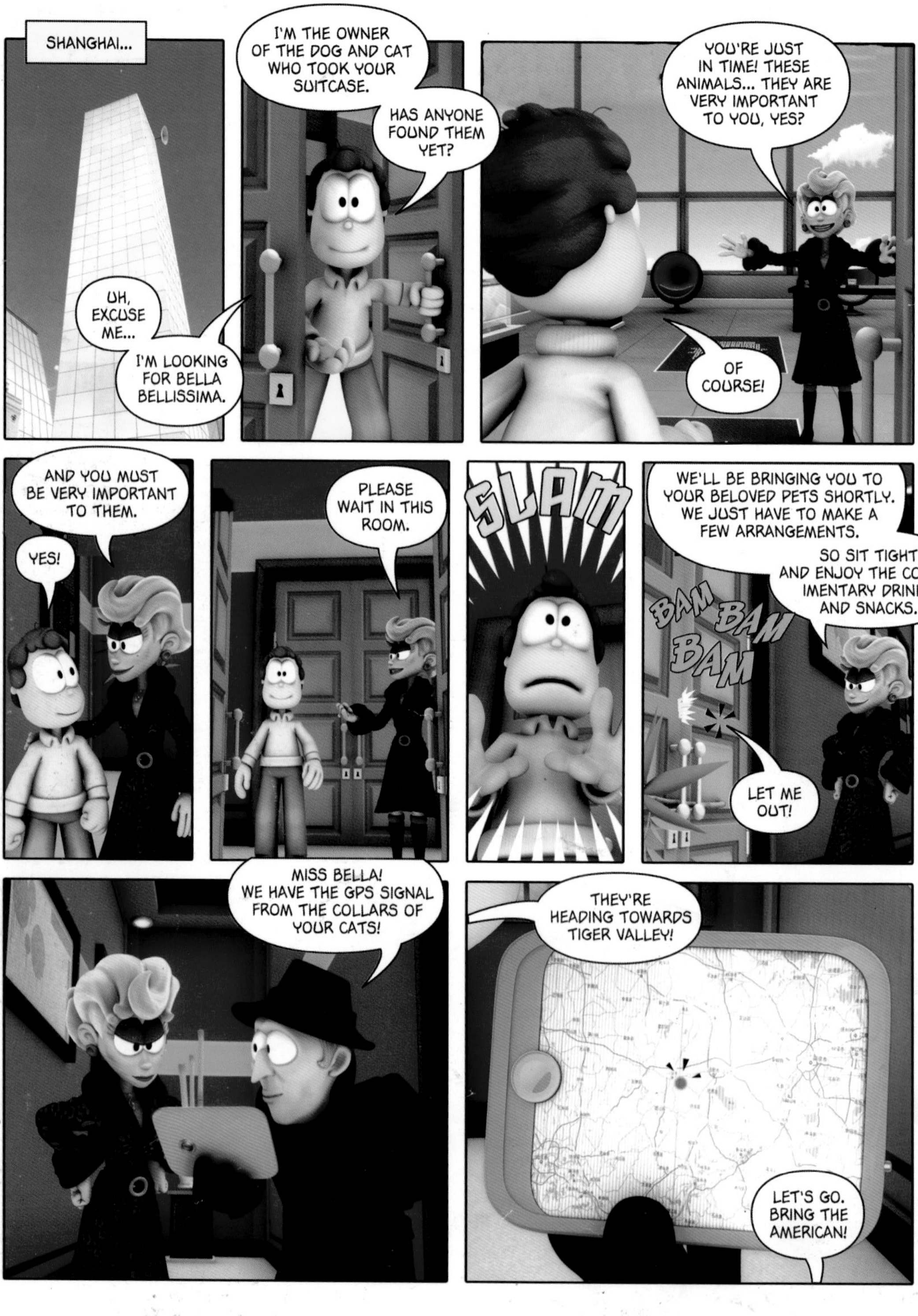

SHANGHAI...
UH, EXCUSE ME...
I'M LOOKING FOR BELLA BELLISSIMA.
I'M THE OWNER OF THE DOG AND CAT WHO TOOK YOUR SUITCASE.
HAS ANYONE FOUND THEM YET?
YOU'RE JUST IN TIME! THESE ANIMALS... THEY ARE VERY IMPORTANT TO YOU, YES?
OF COURSE!
AND YOU MUST BE VERY IMPORTANT TO THEM.
YES!
PLEASE WAIT IN THIS ROOM.
SLAM
WE'LL BE BRINGING YOU TO YOUR BELOVED PETS SHORTLY. WE JUST HAVE TO MAKE A FEW ARRANGEMENTS.
SO SIT TIGHT AND ENJOY THE COMPLIMENTARY DRINKS AND SNACKS.
BAM BAM BAM
LET ME OUT!
MISS BELLA! WE HAVE THE GPS SIGNAL FROM THE COLLARS OF YOUR CATS!
THEY'RE HEADING TOWARDS TIGER VALLEY!
LET'S GO. BRING THE AMERICAN!

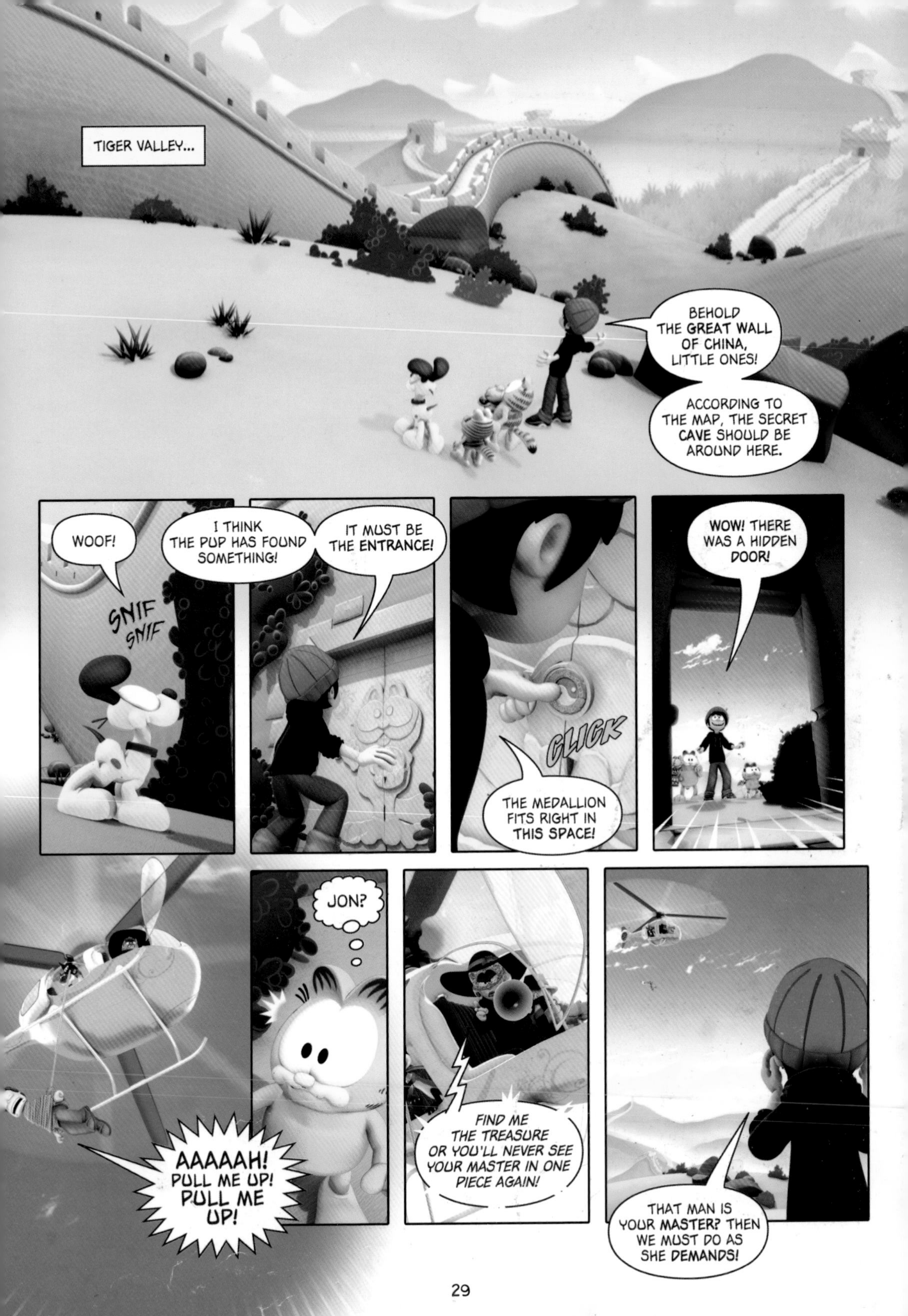
TIGER VALLEY...
BEHOLD THE GREAT WALL OF CHINA, LITTLE ONES!
ACCORDING TO THE MAP, THE SECRET CAVE SHOULD BE AROUND HERE.
WOOF!
SNIF SNIF
I THINK THE PUP HAS FOUND SOMETHING!
IT MUST BE THE ENTRANCE!
CLICK
THE MEDALLION FITS RIGHT IN THIS SPACE!
WOW! THERE WAS A HIDDEN DOOR!
AAAAAH! PULL ME UP! PULL ME UP!
JON?
FIND ME THE TREASURE OR YOU'LL NEVER SEE YOUR MASTER IN ONE PIECE AGAIN!
THAT MAN IS YOUR MASTER? THEN WE MUST DO AS SHE DEMANDS!

YOU'LL HAVE TO EXPLAIN TO ME HOW WE GOT INTO THIS MESS.
HURRY UP!
WHAT'S THIS TREASURE SHE KEEPS YELLING ABOUT?
TREASURE OF FUCANGLONG. TEN-FOOT LONG DRAGON. GUARDS FORBIDDEN RICHES.
SURE, WHY NOT?
WEIRD LIGHT BEAMS CROSSING ROOM. PROBABLY NOT GOOD.
DON'T JUST STAND THERE! KEEP MOVING!
CAREFUL, JON. WE MUSTN'T BREAK THE BEAMS.
IS THIS SOME KIND OF RIDDLE?
THOSE ARE THE TWELVE SIGNS OF THE CHINESE ZODIAC!
WE JUST HAVE TO PUT THEM BACK IN ORDER.
THE BUFFALO THERE AND THEN THE TIGER.
RRRRRRRRRR

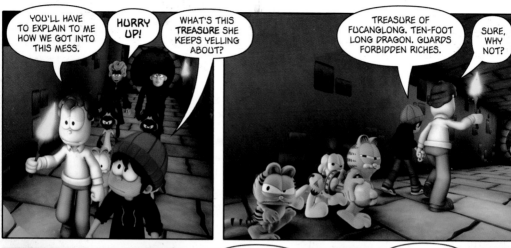

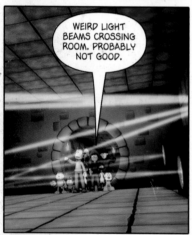

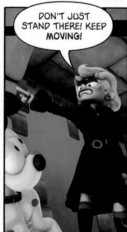

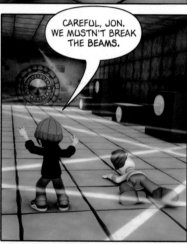

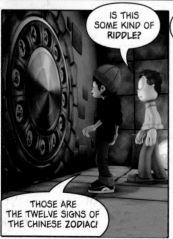

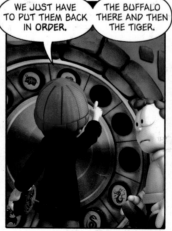

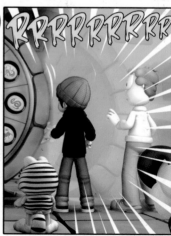

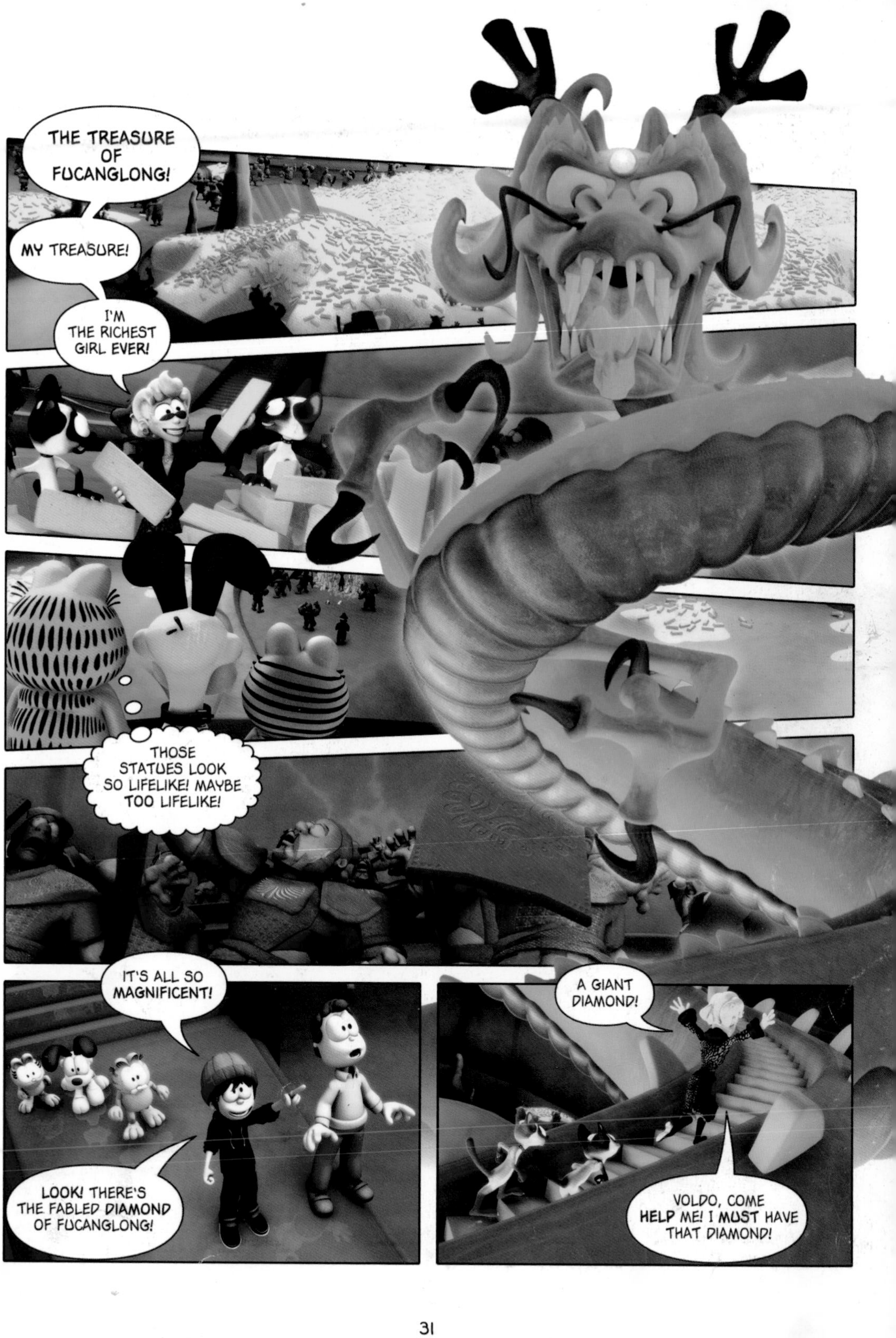
THE TREASURE OF FUCANGLONG!
MY TREASURE!
I'M THE RICHEST GIRL EVER!
THOSE STATUES LOOK SO LIFELIKE! MAYBE TOO LIFELIKE!
IT'S ALL SO MAGNIFICENT!
LOOK! THERE'S THE FABLED DIAMOND OF FUCANGLONG!
A GIANT DIAMOND!
VOLDO, COME HELP ME! I MUST HAVE THAT DIAMOND!

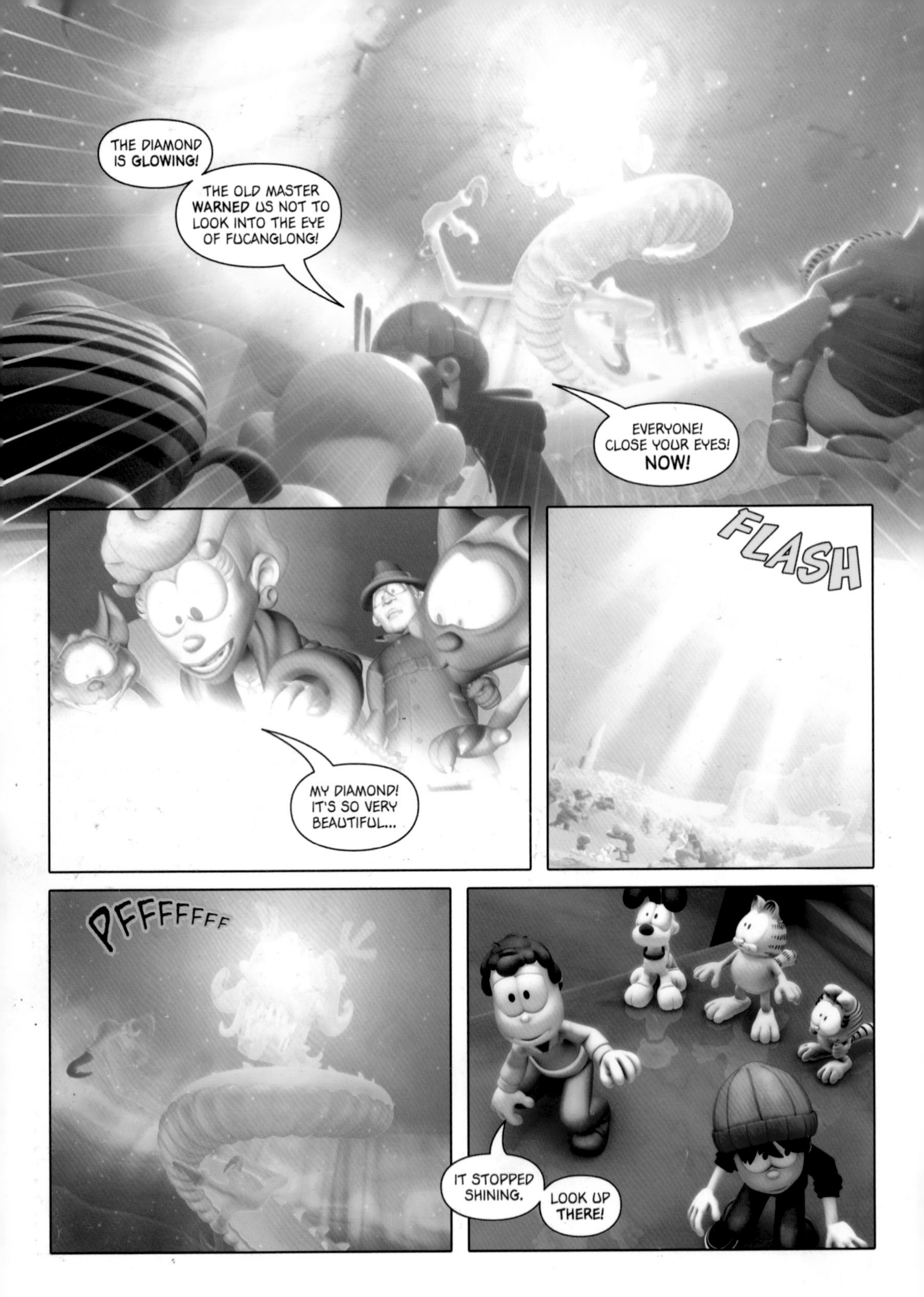

THE DIAMOND IS GLOWING!
THE OLD MASTER WARNED US NOT TO LOOK INTO THE EYE OF FUCANGLONG!
EVERYONE! CLOSE YOUR EYES! NOW!
MY DIAMOND! IT'S SO VERY BEAUTIFUL...
FLASH
PFFFFFFF
IT STOPPED SHINING.
LOOK UP THERE!

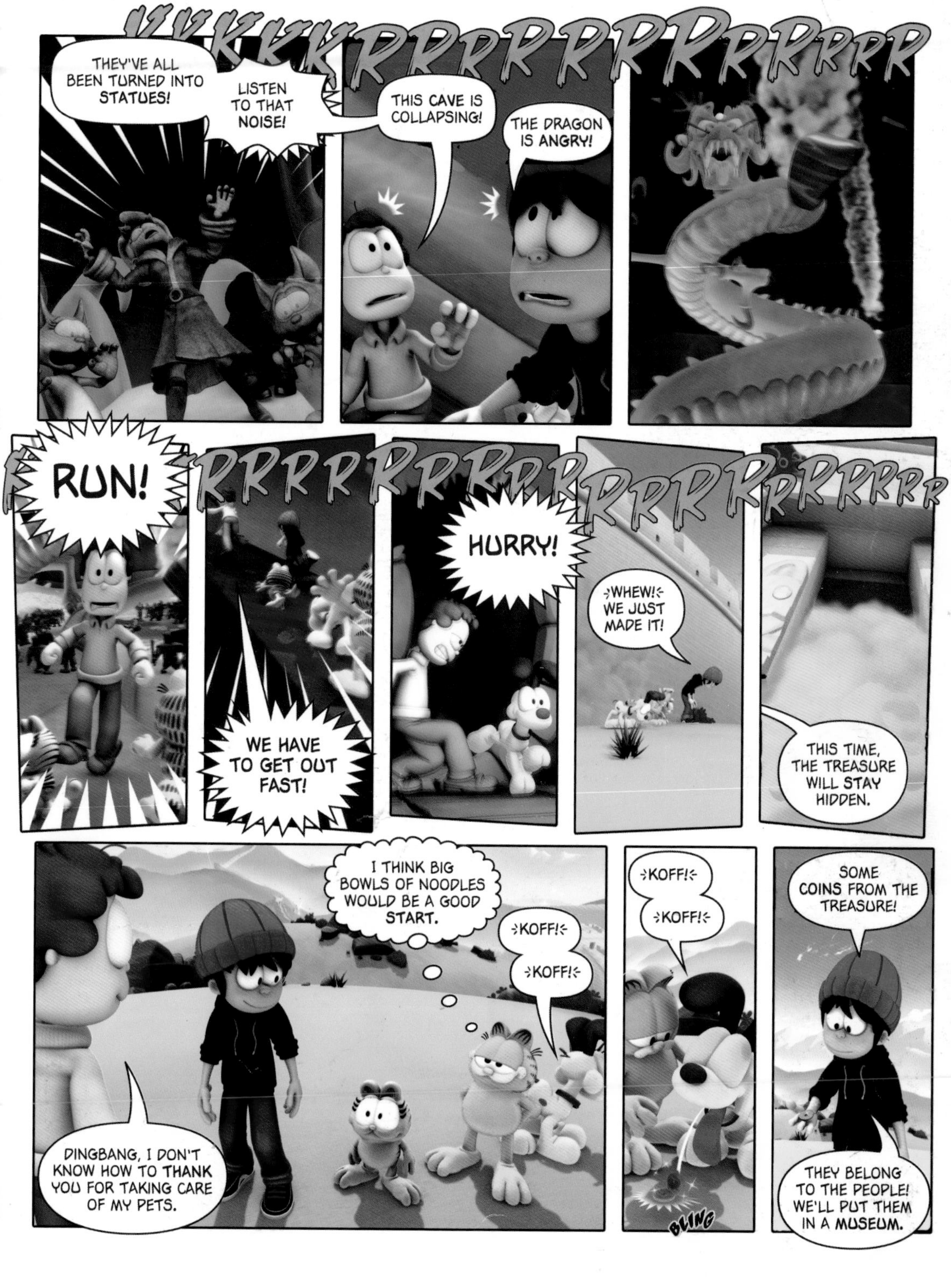
THEY'VE ALL BEEN TURNED INTO STATUES!
LISTEN TO THAT NOISE!
THIS CAVE IS COLLAPSING!
THE DRAGON IS ANGRY!
RUN!
WE HAVE TO GET OUT FAST!
HURRY!
WHEW! WE JUST MADE IT!
THIS TIME, THE TREASURE WILL STAY HIDDEN.
DINGBANG, I DON'T KNOW HOW TO THANK YOU FOR TAKING CARE OF MY PETS.
I THINK BIG BOWLS OF NOODLES WOULD BE A GOOD START.
KOFF!
KOFF!
KOFF!
KOFF!
BLING
SOME COINS FROM THE TREASURE!
THEY BELONG TO THE PEOPLE! WE'LL PUT THEM IN A MUSEUM.

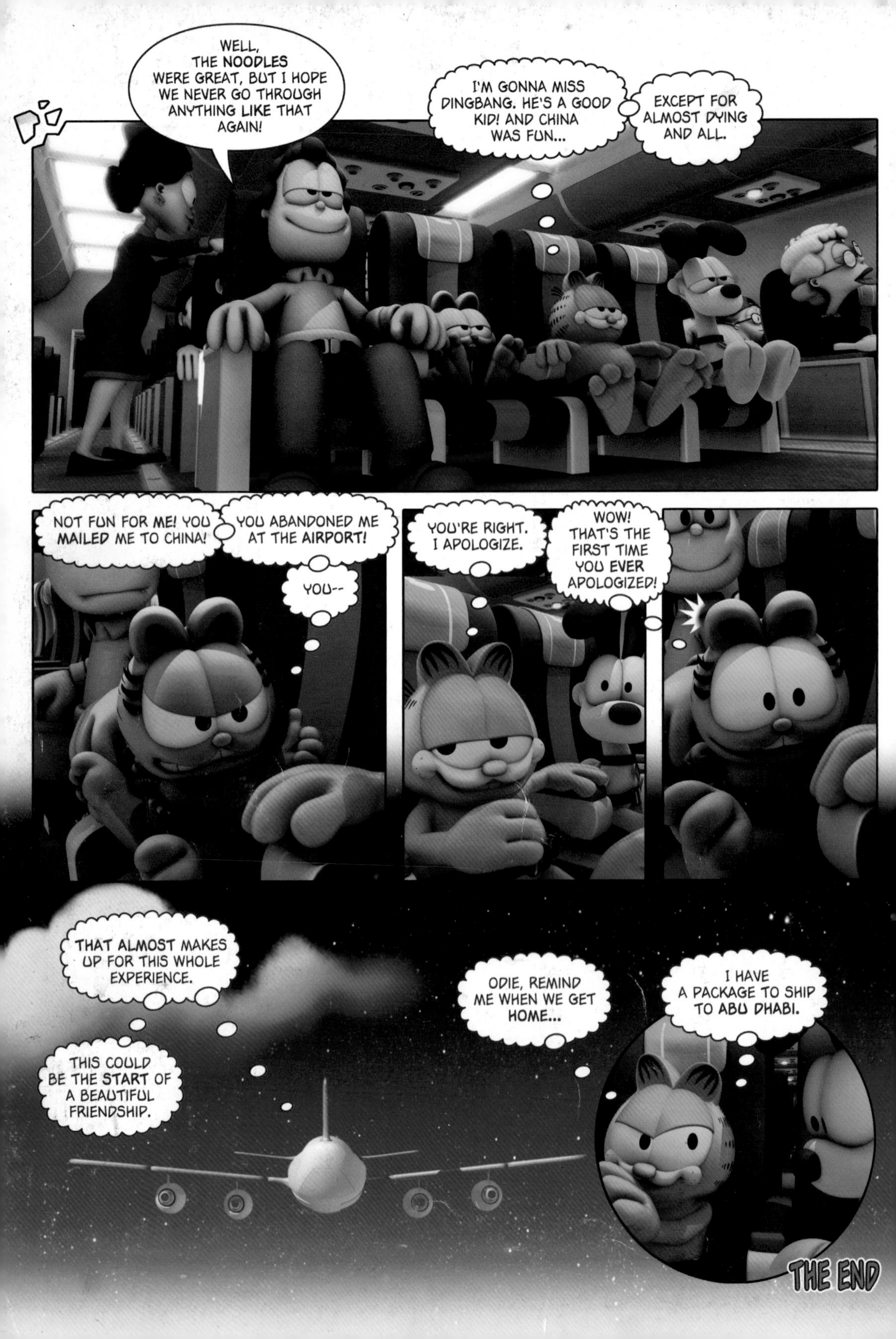
WELL, THE NOODLES WERE GREAT, BUT I HOPE WE NEVER GO THROUGH ANYTHING LIKE THAT AGAIN!
I'M GONNA MISS DINGBANG. HE'S A GOOD KID! AND CHINA WAS FUN...
EXCEPT FOR ALMOST DYING AND ALL.
NOT FUN FOR ME! YOU MAILED ME TO CHINA!
YOU ABANDONED ME AT THE AIRPORT!
YOU--
YOU'RE RIGHT. I APOLOGIZE.
WOW! THAT'S THE FIRST TIME YOU EVER APOLOGIZED!
THAT ALMOST MAKES UP FOR THIS WHOLE EXPERIENCE.
THIS COULD BE THE START OF A BEAUTIFUL FRIENDSHIP.
ODIE, REMIND ME WHEN WE GET HOME...
I HAVE A PACKAGE TO SHIP TO ABU DHABI.
THE END

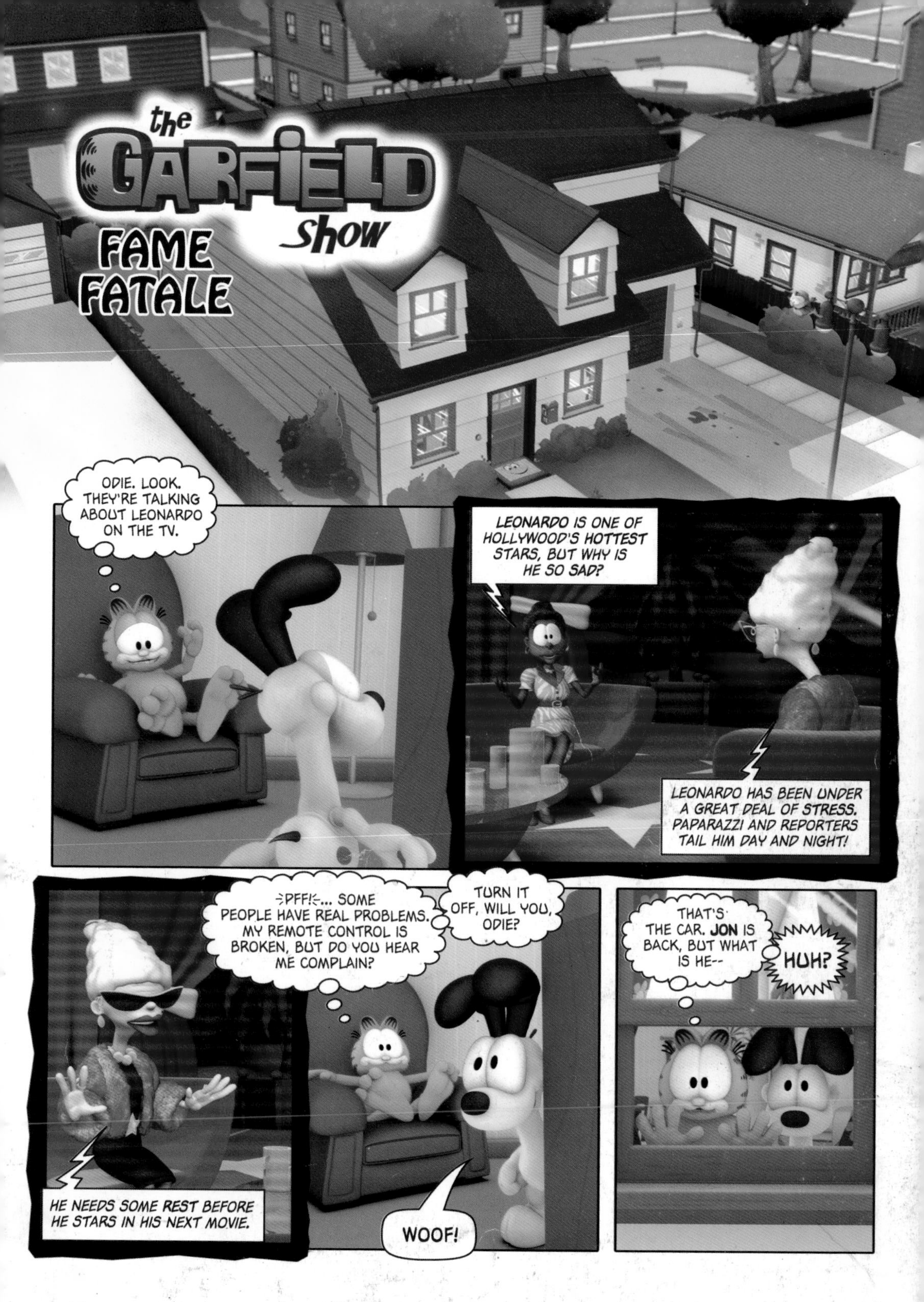
the GARFIELD show
FAME FATALE
ODIE. LOOK. THEY'RE TALKING ABOUT LEONARDO ON THE TV.
LEONARDO IS ONE OF HOLLYWOOD'S HOTTEST STARS, BUT WHY IS HE SO SAD?
LEONARDO HAS BEEN UNDER A GREAT DEAL OF STRESS. PAPARAZZI AND REPORTERS TAIL HIM DAY AND NIGHT!
HE NEEDS SOME REST BEFORE HE STARS IN HIS NEXT MOVIE.
PFFF!... SOME PEOPLE HAVE REAL PROBLEMS. MY REMOTE CONTROL IS BROKEN, BUT DO YOU HEAR ME COMPLAIN?
TURN IT OFF, WILL YOU, ODIE?
WOOF!
THAT'S THE CAR. JON IS BACK, BUT WHAT IS HE--
HUH?

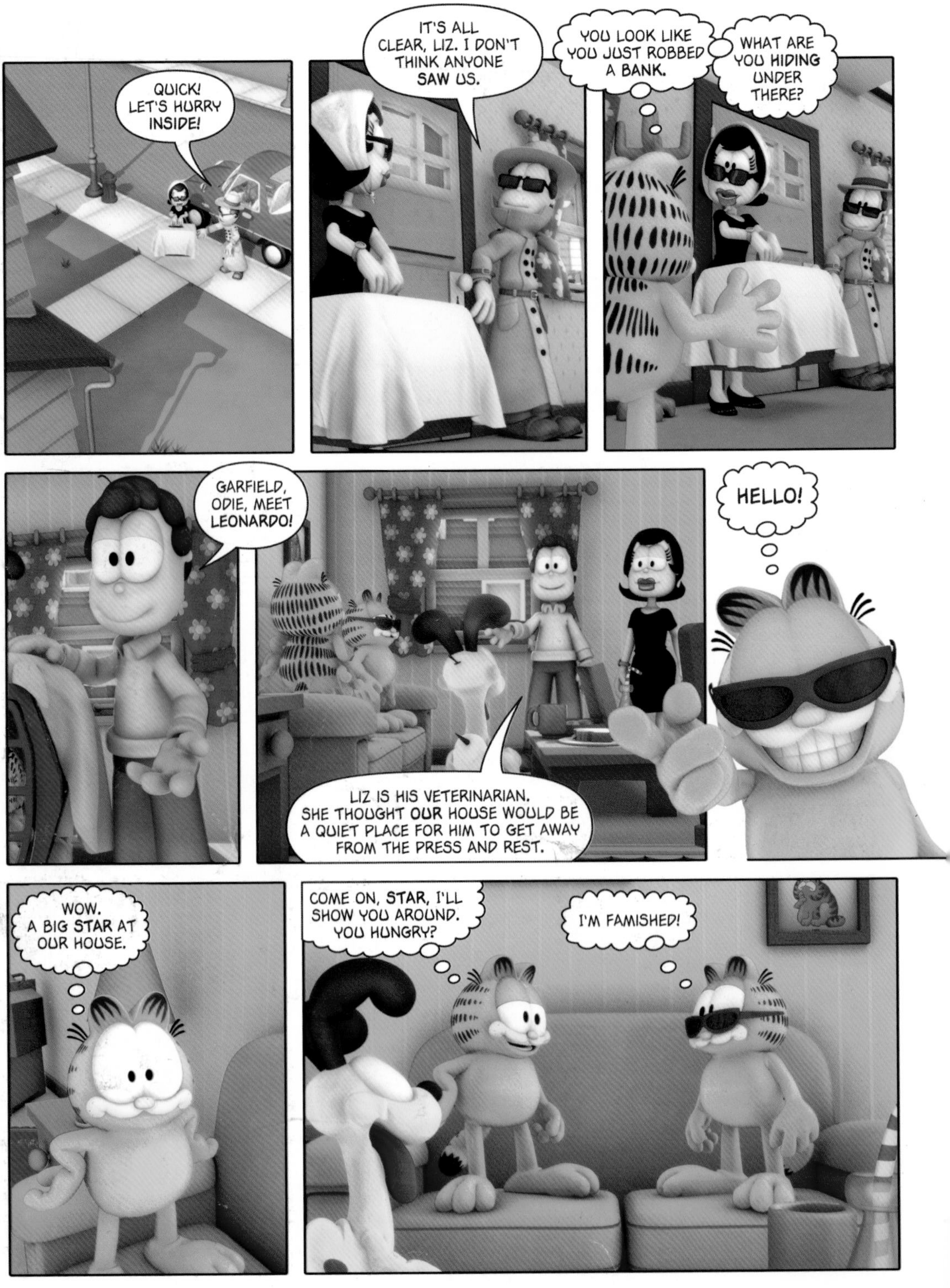
QUICK! LET'S HURRY INSIDE!
IT'S ALL CLEAR, LIZ. I DON'T THINK ANYONE SAW US.
YOU LOOK LIKE YOU JUST ROBBED A BANK.
WHAT ARE YOU HIDING UNDER THERE?
GARFIELD, ODIE, MEET LEONARDO!
LIZ IS HIS VETERINARIAN. SHE THOUGHT OUR HOUSE WOULD BE A QUIET PLACE FOR HIM TO GET AWAY FROM THE PRESS AND REST.
HELLO!
WOW. A BIG STAR AT OUR HOUSE.
COME ON, STAR, I'LL SHOW YOU AROUND. YOU HUNGRY?
I'M FAMISHED!

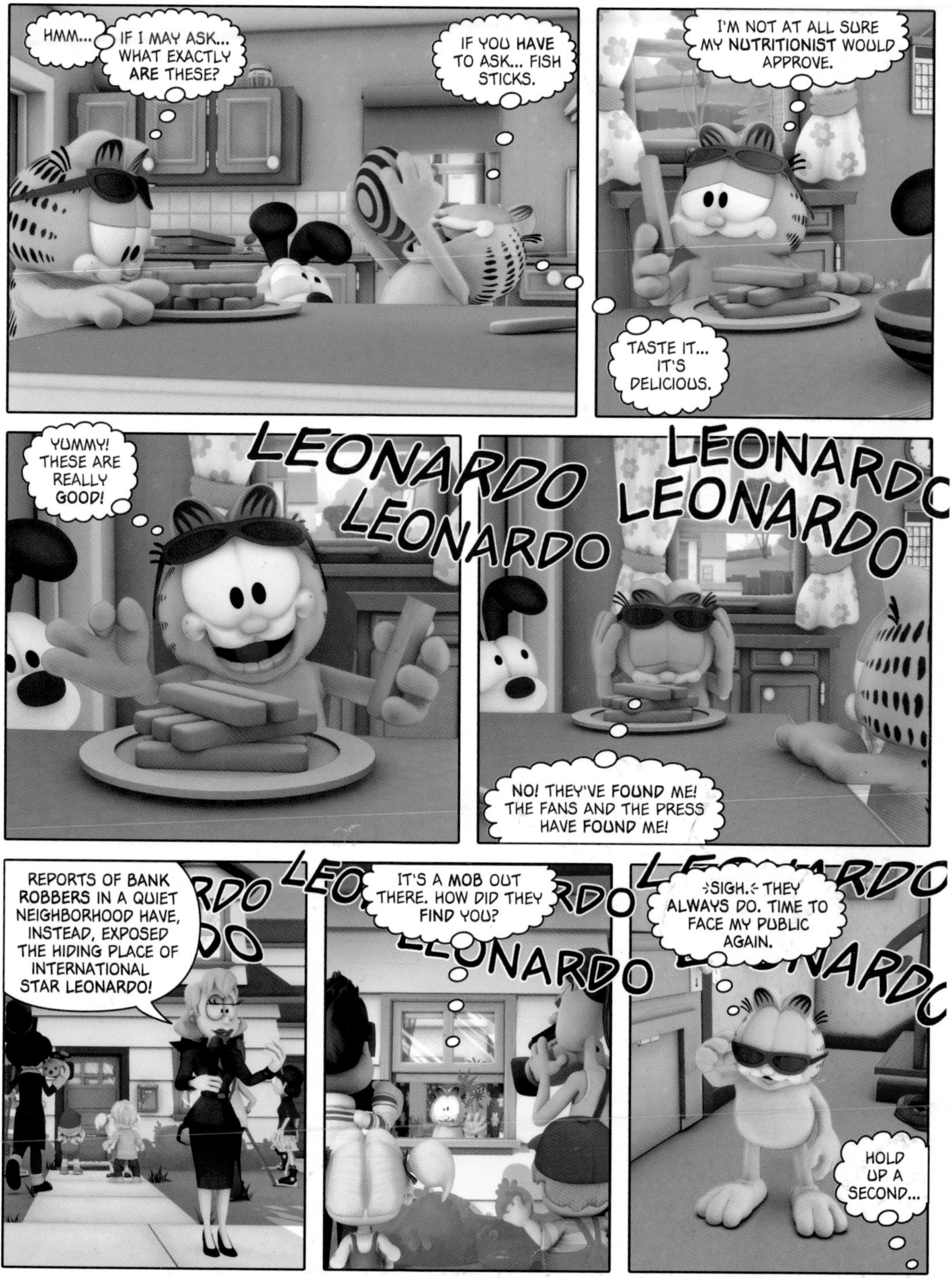
HMM...
IF I MAY ASK... WHAT EXACTLY ARE THESE?
IF YOU HAVE TO ASK... FISH STICKS.
I'M NOT AT ALL SURE MY NUTRITIONIST WOULD APPROVE.
TASTE IT... IT'S DELICIOUS.
YUMMY! THESE ARE REALLY GOOD!
LEONARDO
LEONARDO
LEONARDO
LEONARDO
LEONARDO
NO! THEY'VE FOUND ME! THE FANS AND THE PRESS HAVE FOUND ME!
REPORTS OF BANK ROBBERS IN A QUIET NEIGHBORHOOD HAVE, INSTEAD, EXPOSED THE HIDING PLACE OF INTERNATIONAL STAR LEONARDO!
IT'S A MOB OUT THERE. HOW DID THEY FIND YOU?
SIGH. THEY ALWAYS DO. TIME TO FACE MY PUBLIC AGAIN.
HOLD UP A SECOND...

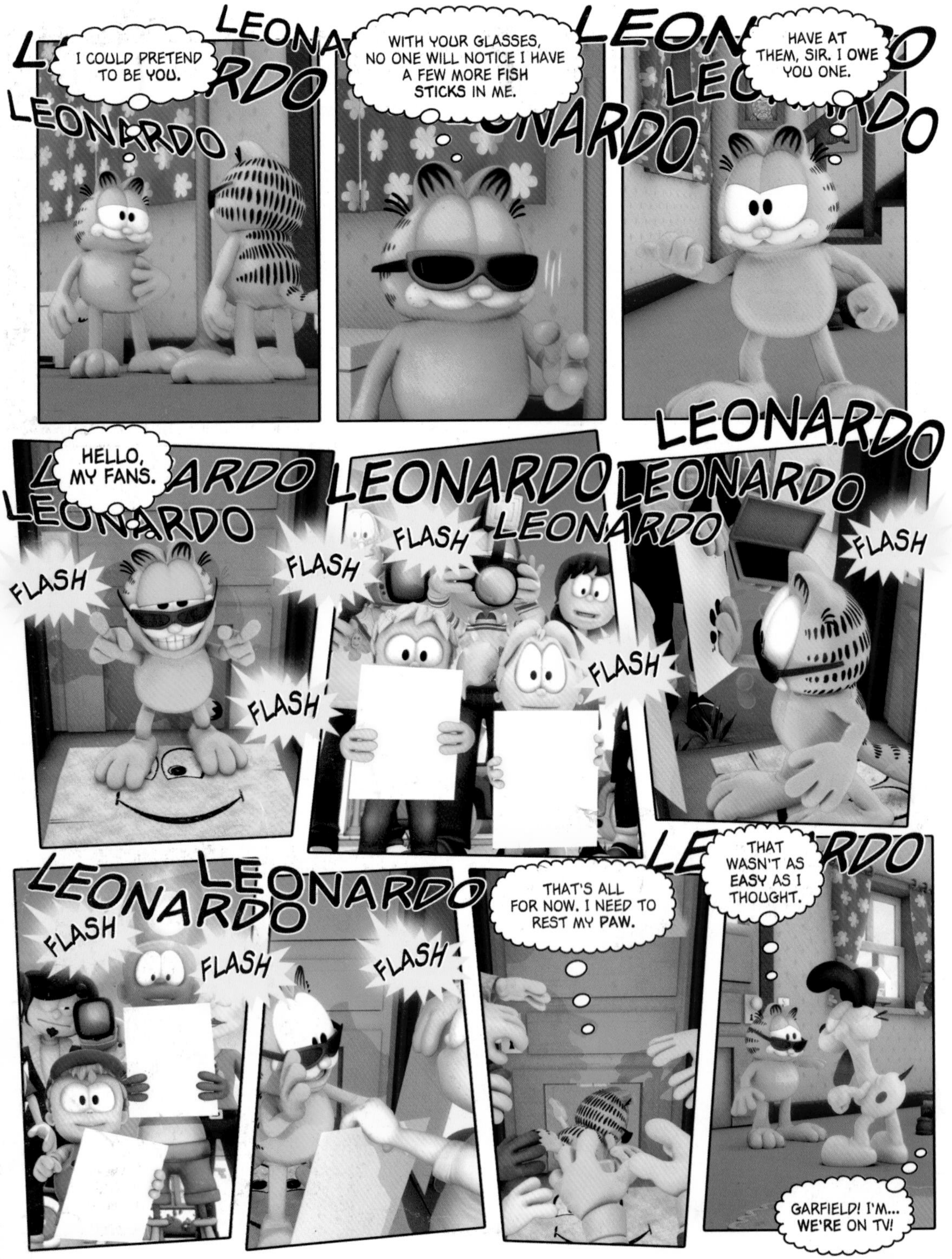
LEONARDO
I COULD PRETEND TO BE YOU.
WITH YOUR GLASSES, NO ONE WILL NOTICE I HAVE A FEW MORE FISH STICKS IN ME.
HAVE AT THEM, SIR. I OWE YOU ONE.
LEONARDO
HELLO, MY FANS.
LEONARDO
FLASH
FLASH
LEONARDO
FLASH
FLASH
LEONARDO
LEONARDO
FLASH
FLASH
LEONARDO
FLASH
FLASH
FLASH
THAT'S ALL FOR NOW. I NEED TO REST MY PAW.
THAT WASN'T AS EASY AS I THOUGHT.
GARFIELD! I'M... WE'RE ON TV!

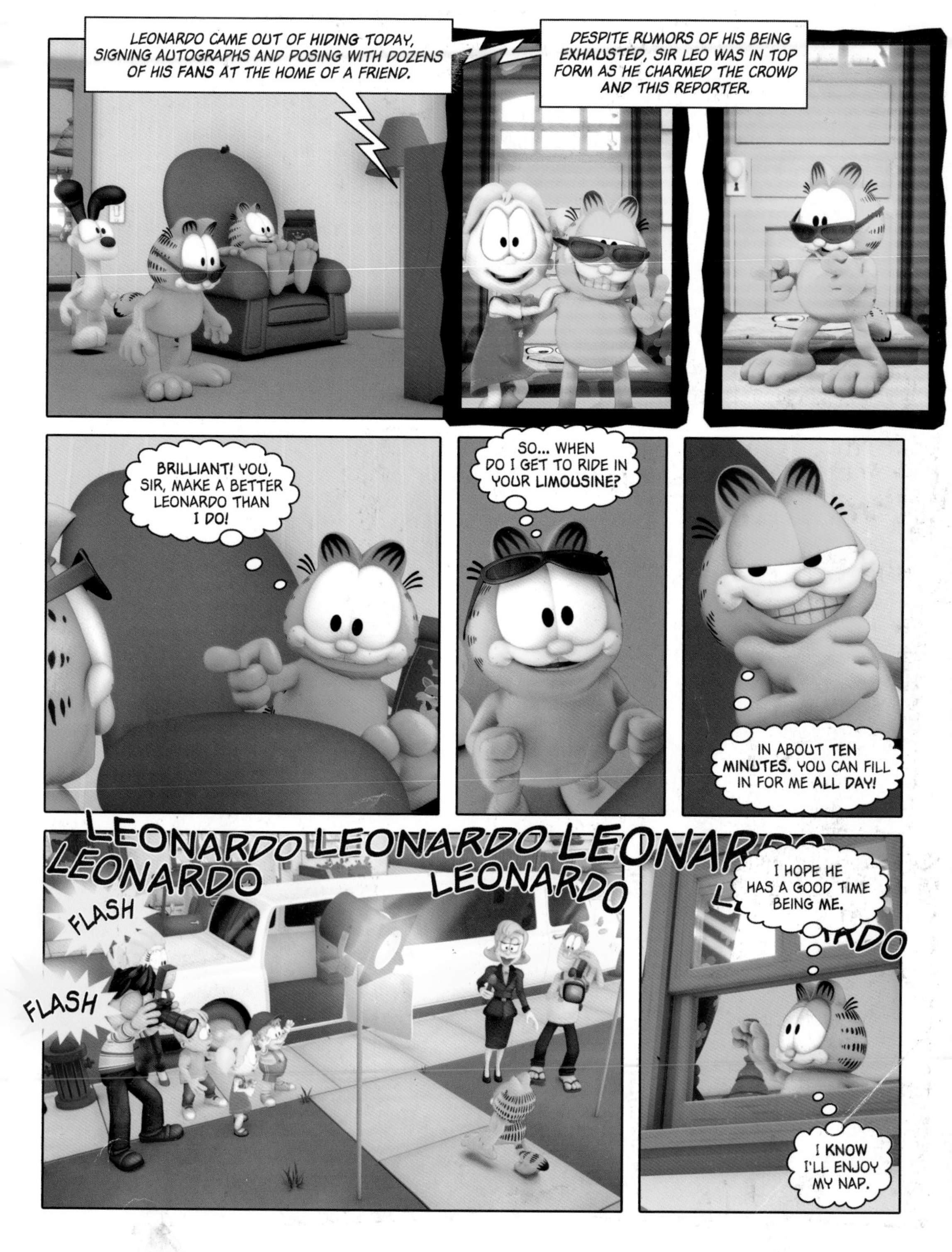
LEONARDO CAME OUT OF HIDING TODAY, SIGNING AUTOGRAPHS AND POSING WITH DOZENS OF HIS FANS AT THE HOME OF A FRIEND.
DESPITE RUMORS OF HIS BEING EXHAUSTED, SIR LEO WAS IN TOP FORM AS HE CHARMED THE CROWD AND THIS REPORTER.
BRILLIANT! YOU, SIR, MAKE A BETTER LEONARDO THAN I DO!
SO... WHEN DO I GET TO RIDE IN YOUR LIMOUSINE?
IN ABOUT TEN MINUTES. YOU CAN FILL IN FOR ME ALL DAY!
LEONARDO LEONARDO LEONARDO
LEONARDO
LEONARDO
FLASH
FLASH
I HOPE HE HAS A GOOD TIME BEING ME.
I KNOW I'LL ENJOY MY NAP.

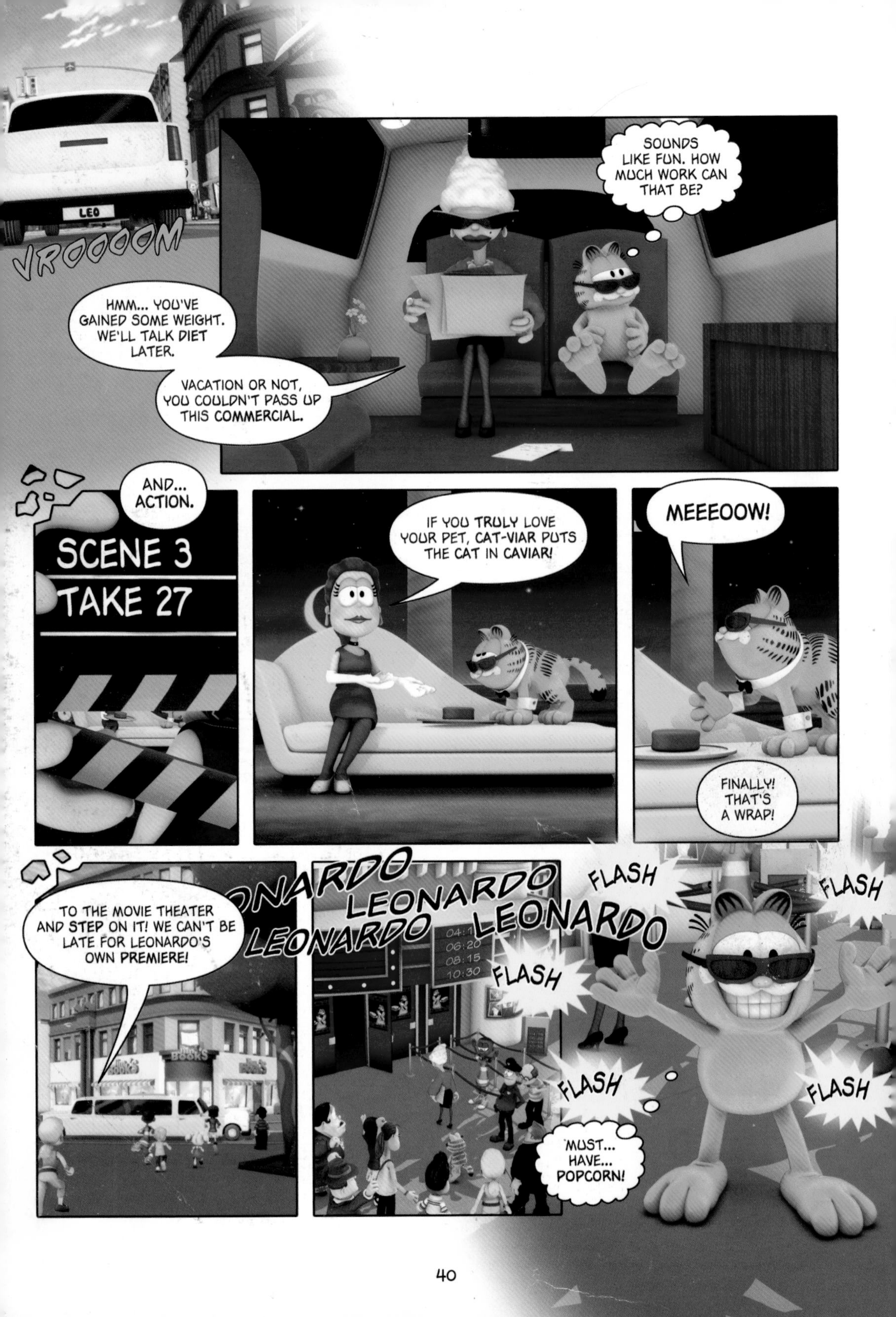

VROOOOM
SOUNDS LIKE FUN. HOW MUCH WORK CAN THAT BE?
HMM... YOU'VE GAINED SOME WEIGHT. WE'LL TALK DIET LATER.
VACATION OR NOT, YOU COULDN'T PASS UP THIS COMMERCIAL.
AND... ACTION.
SCENE 3
TAKE 27
IF YOU TRULY LOVE YOUR PET, CAT-VIAR PUTS THE CAT IN CAVIAR!
MEEEOOW!
FINALLY! THAT'S A WRAP!
TO THE MOVIE THEATER AND STEP ON IT! WE CAN'T BE LATE FOR LEONARDO'S OWN PREMIERE!
LEONARDO
LEONARDO
LEONARDO
FLASH
FLASH
FLASH
FLASH
FLASH
MUST... HAVE... POPCORN!

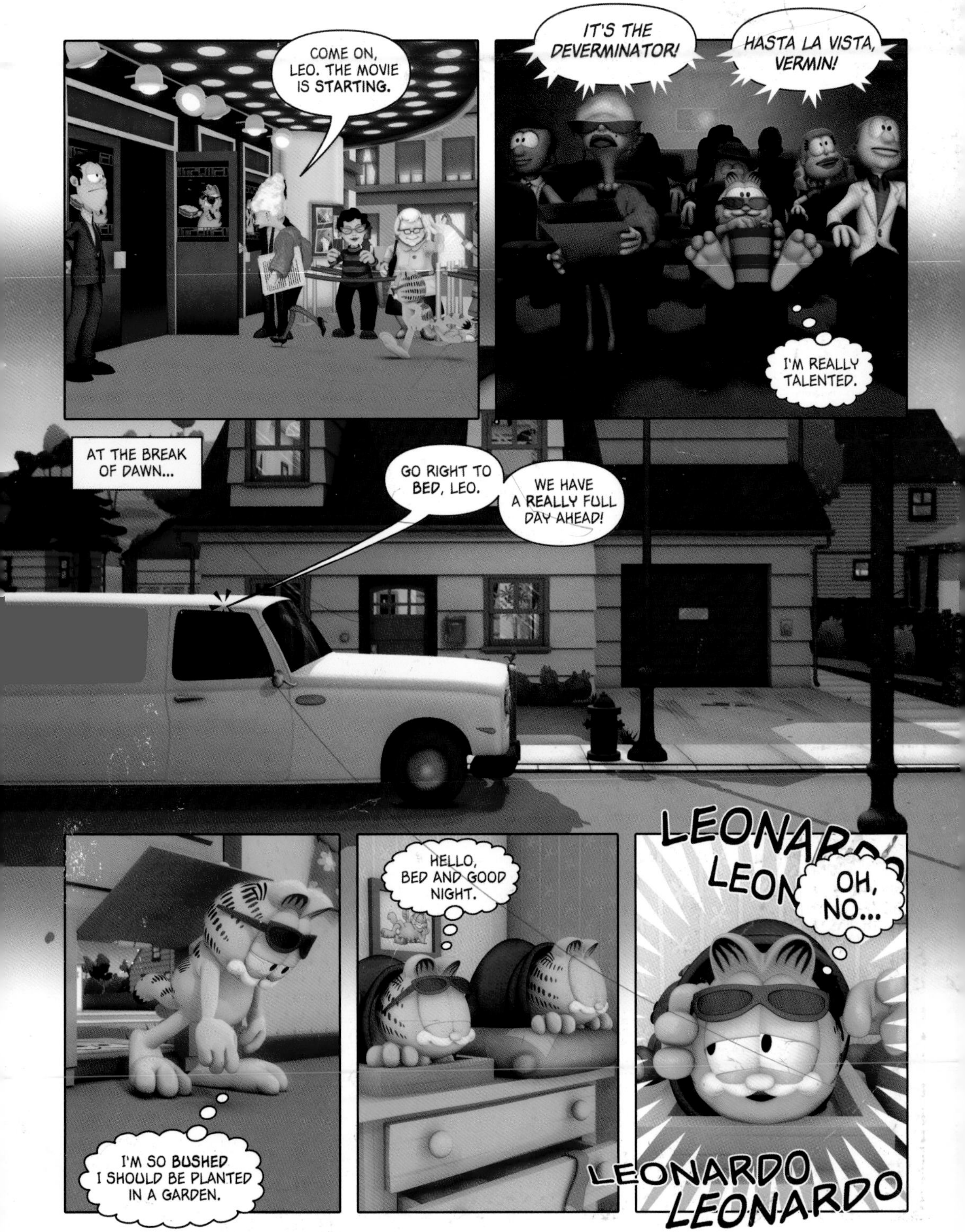
COME ON, LEO. THE MOVIE IS STARTING.
IT'S THE DEVERMINATOR!
HASTA LA VISTA, VERMIN!
I'M REALLY TALENTED.
AT THE BREAK OF DAWN...
GO RIGHT TO BED, LEO.
WE HAVE A REALLY FULL DAY AHEAD!
I'M SO BUSHED I SHOULD BE PLANTED IN A GARDEN.
HELLO, BED AND GOOD NIGHT.
OH, NO...
LEONARDO
LEONARDO

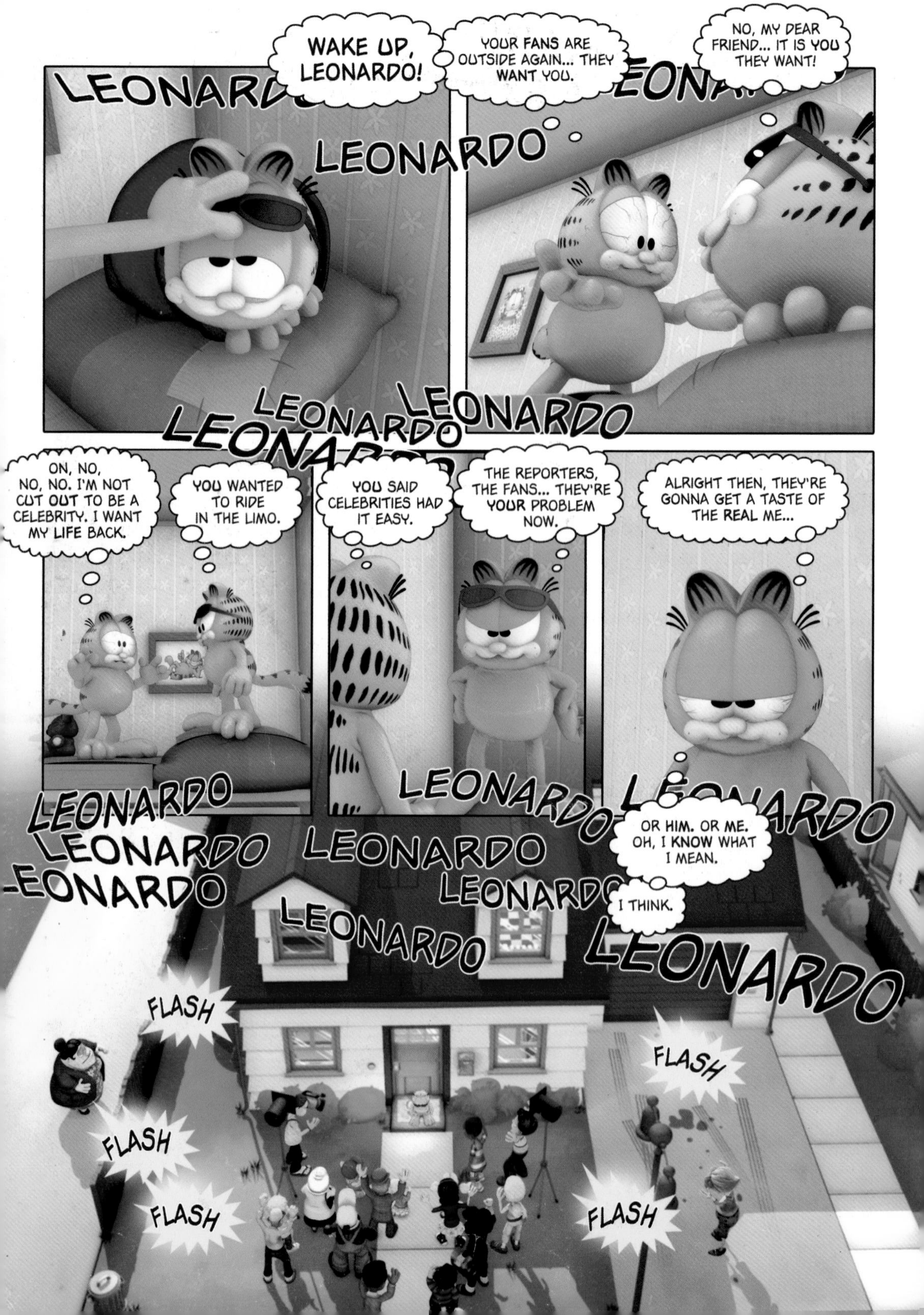

WAKE UP, LEONARDO!
YOUR FANS ARE OUTSIDE AGAIN... THEY WANT YOU.
NO, MY DEAR FRIEND... IT IS YOU THEY WANT!
LEONARDO
LEONARDO
LEONARDO
LEONARDO
ON, NO, NO, NO. I'M NOT CUT OUT TO BE A CELEBRITY. I WANT MY LIFE BACK.
YOU WANTED TO RIDE IN THE LIMO.
YOU SAID CELEBRITIES HAD IT EASY.
THE REPORTERS, THE FANS... THEY'RE YOUR PROBLEM NOW.
ALRIGHT THEN, THEY'RE GONNA GET A TASTE OF THE REAL ME...
OR HIM. OR ME. OH, I KNOW WHAT I MEAN.
I THINK.
LEONARDO
LEONARDO
LEONARDO
LEONARDO
LEONARDO
LEONARDO
FLASH
FLASH
FLASH
FLASH
FLASH

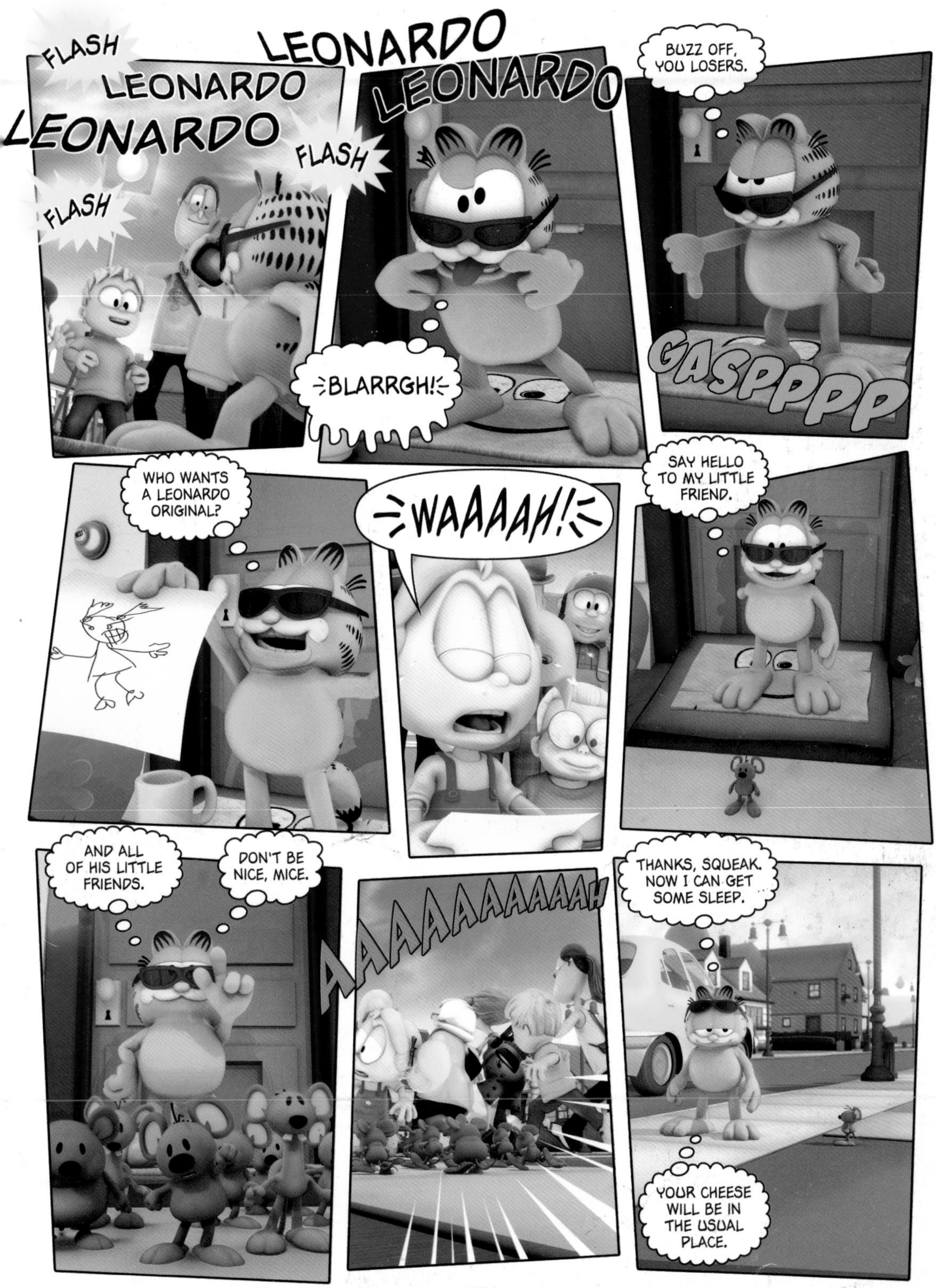
FLASH
LEONARDO
LEONARDO
LEONARDO
FLASH
FLASH
LEONARDO
BLARRGH!
BUZZ OFF, YOU LOSERS.
GASPPPPP
WHO WANTS A LEONARDO ORIGINAL?
WAAAAH!
SAY HELLO TO MY LITTLE FRIEND.
AND ALL OF HIS LITTLE FRIENDS.
DON'T BE NICE, MICE.
AAAAAAAAAAAH
THANKS, SQUEAK. NOW I CAN GET SOME SLEEP.
YOUR CHEESE WILL BE IN THE USUAL PLACE.

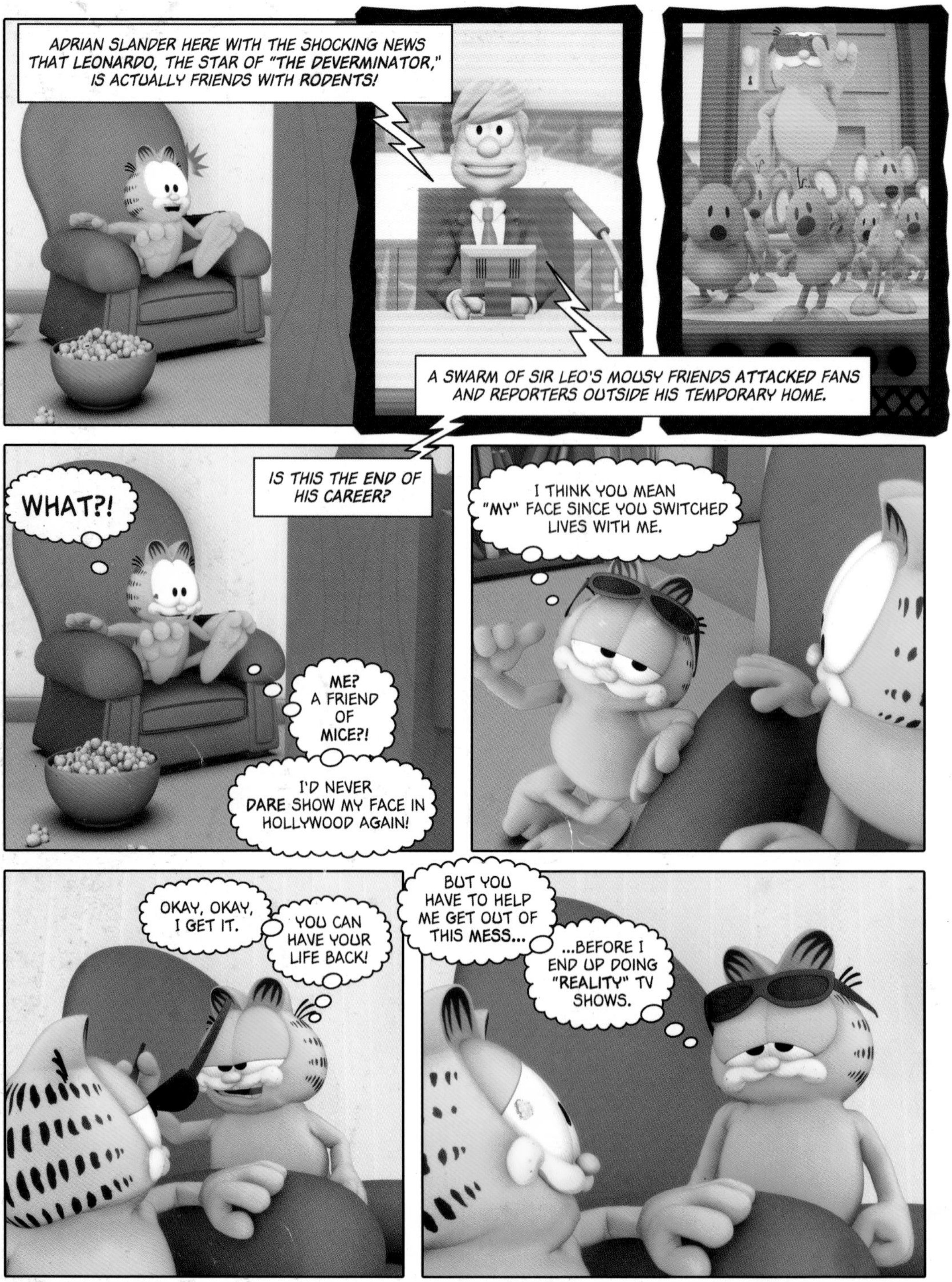
ADRIAN SLANDER HERE WITH THE SHOCKING NEWS THAT LEONARDO, THE STAR OF "THE DEVERMINATOR," IS ACTUALLY FRIENDS WITH RODENTS!
A SWARM OF SIR LEO'S MOUSY FRIENDS ATTACKED FANS AND REPORTERS OUTSIDE HIS TEMPORARY HOME.
IS THIS THE END OF HIS CAREER?
WHAT?!
ME? A FRIEND OF MICE?!
I'D NEVER DARE SHOW MY FACE IN HOLLYWOOD AGAIN!
I THINK YOU MEAN "MY" FACE SINCE YOU SWITCHED LIVES WITH ME.
OKAY, OKAY, I GET IT.
YOU CAN HAVE YOUR LIFE BACK!
BUT YOU HAVE TO HELP ME GET OUT OF THIS MESS...
...BEFORE I END UP DOING "REALITY" TV SHOWS.

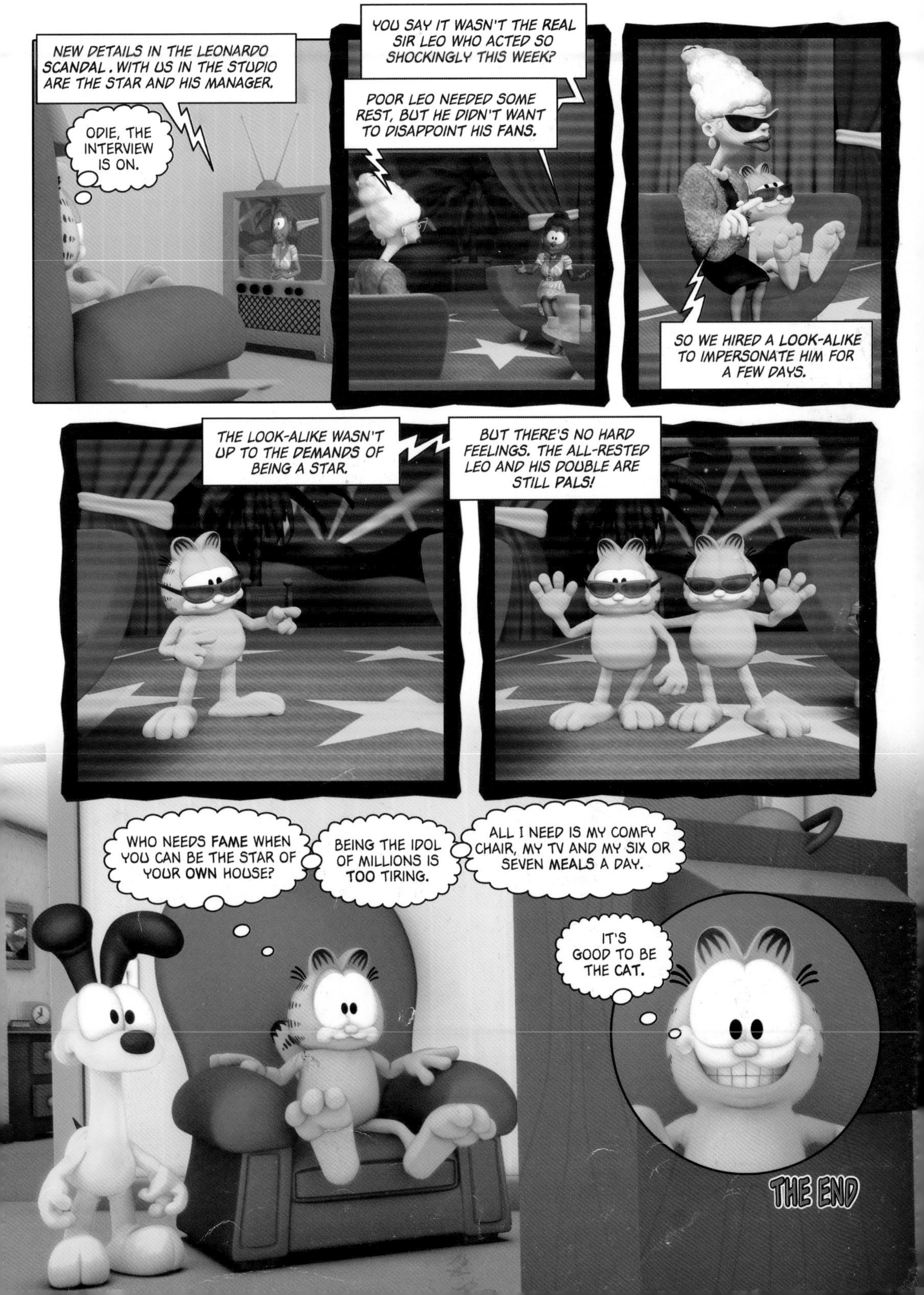
NEW DETAILS IN THE LEONARDO SCANDAL. WITH US IN THE STUDIO ARE THE STAR AND HIS MANAGER.
ODIE, THE INTERVIEW IS ON.
YOU SAY IT WASN'T THE REAL SIR LEO WHO ACTED SO SHOCKINGLY THIS WEEK?
POOR LEO NEEDED SOME REST, BUT HE DIDN'T WANT TO DISAPPOINT HIS FANS.
SO WE HIRED A LOOK-ALIKE TO IMPERSONATE HIM FOR A FEW DAYS.
THE LOOK-ALIKE WASN'T UP TO THE DEMANDS OF BEING A STAR.
BUT THERE'S NO HARD FEELINGS. THE ALL-RESTED LEO AND HIS DOUBLE ARE STILL PALS!
WHO NEEDS FAME WHEN YOU CAN BE THE STAR OF YOUR OWN HOUSE?
BEING THE IDOL OF MILLIONS IS TOO TIRING.
ALL I NEED IS MY COMFY CHAIR, MY TV AND MY SIX OR SEVEN MEALS A DAY.
IT'S GOOD TO BE THE CAT.
THE END

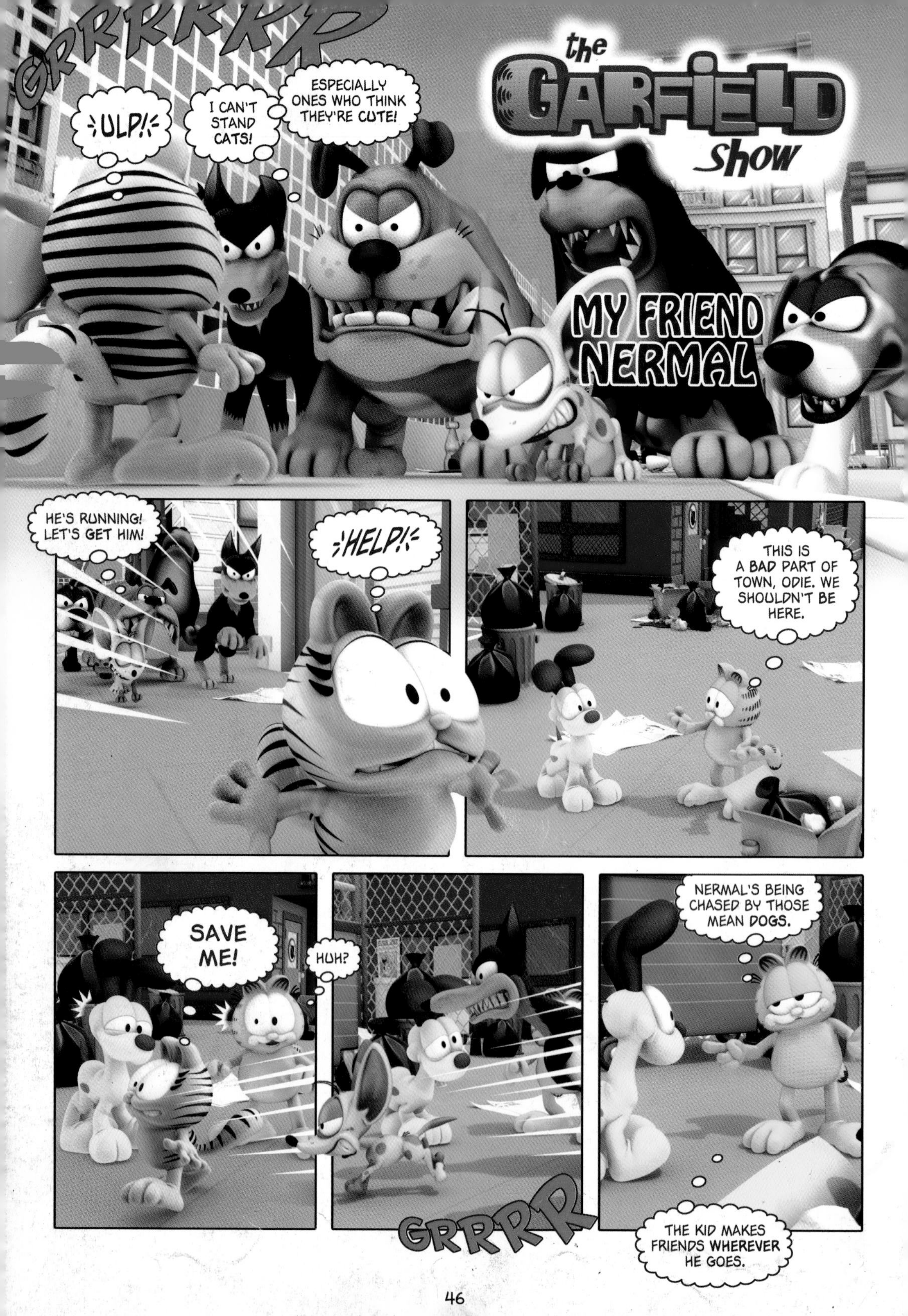
GRRRKKR
the GARFIELD show
MY FRIEND NERMAL
ULP!
I CAN'T STAND CATS!
ESPECIALLY ONES WHO THINK THEY'RE CUTE!
HE'S RUNNING! LET'S GET HIM!
HELP!
THIS IS A BAD PART OF TOWN, ODIE. WE SHOULDN'T BE HERE.
SAVE ME!
HUH?
GRRRR
NERMAL'S BEING CHASED BY THOSE MEAN DOGS.
THE KID MAKES FRIENDS WHEREVER HE GOES.

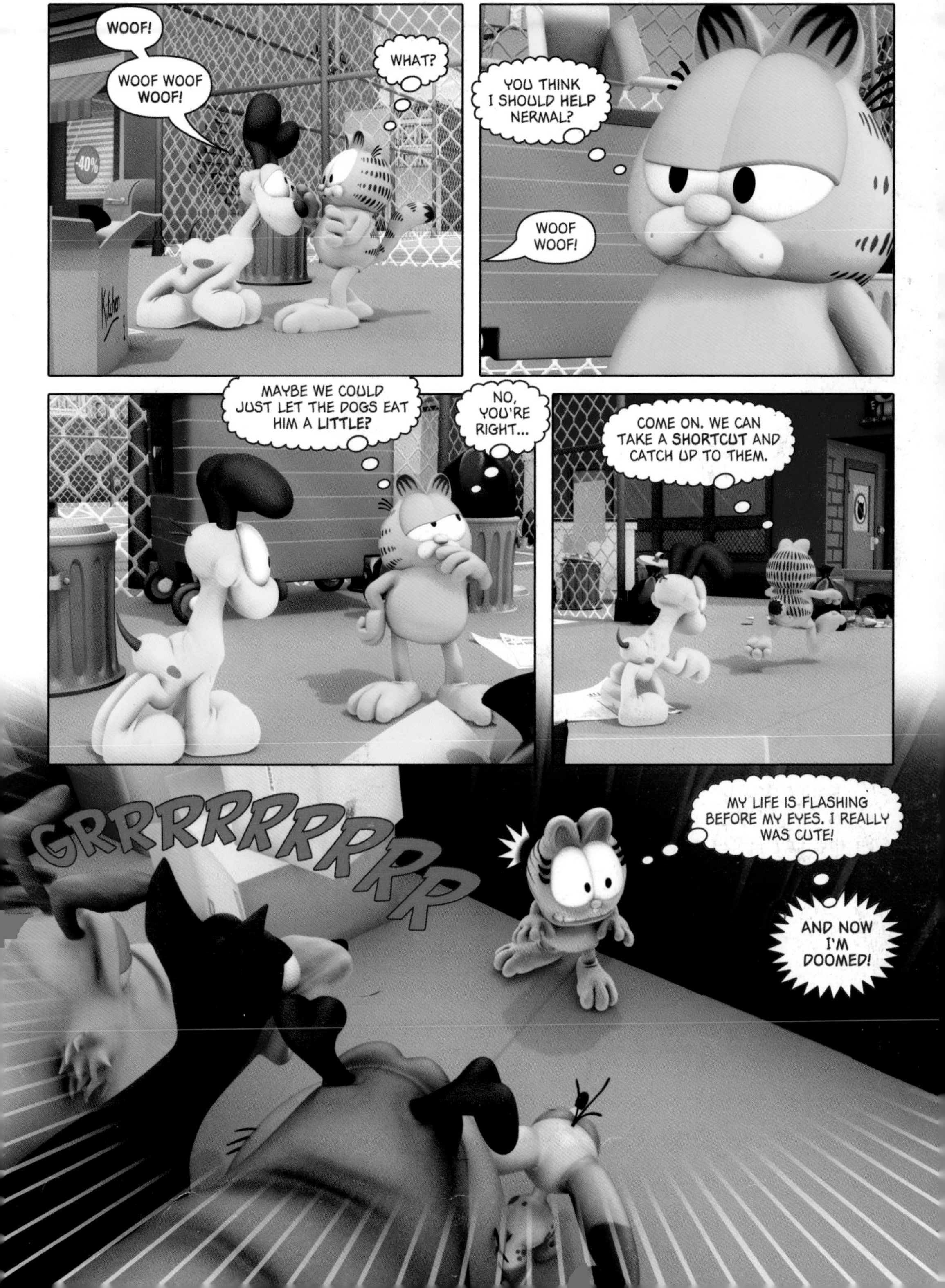
WOOF!
WOOF WOOF WOOF!
WHAT?
-40%
Kitchen
YOU THINK I SHOULD HELP NERMAL?
WOOF WOOF!
MAYBE WE COULD JUST LET THE DOGS EAT HIM A LITTLE?
NO, YOU'RE RIGHT...
COME ON. WE CAN TAKE A SHORTCUT AND CATCH UP TO THEM.
GRRRRRRRRR
MY LIFE IS FLASHING BEFORE MY EYES. I REALLY WAS CUTE!
AND NOW I'M DOOMED!

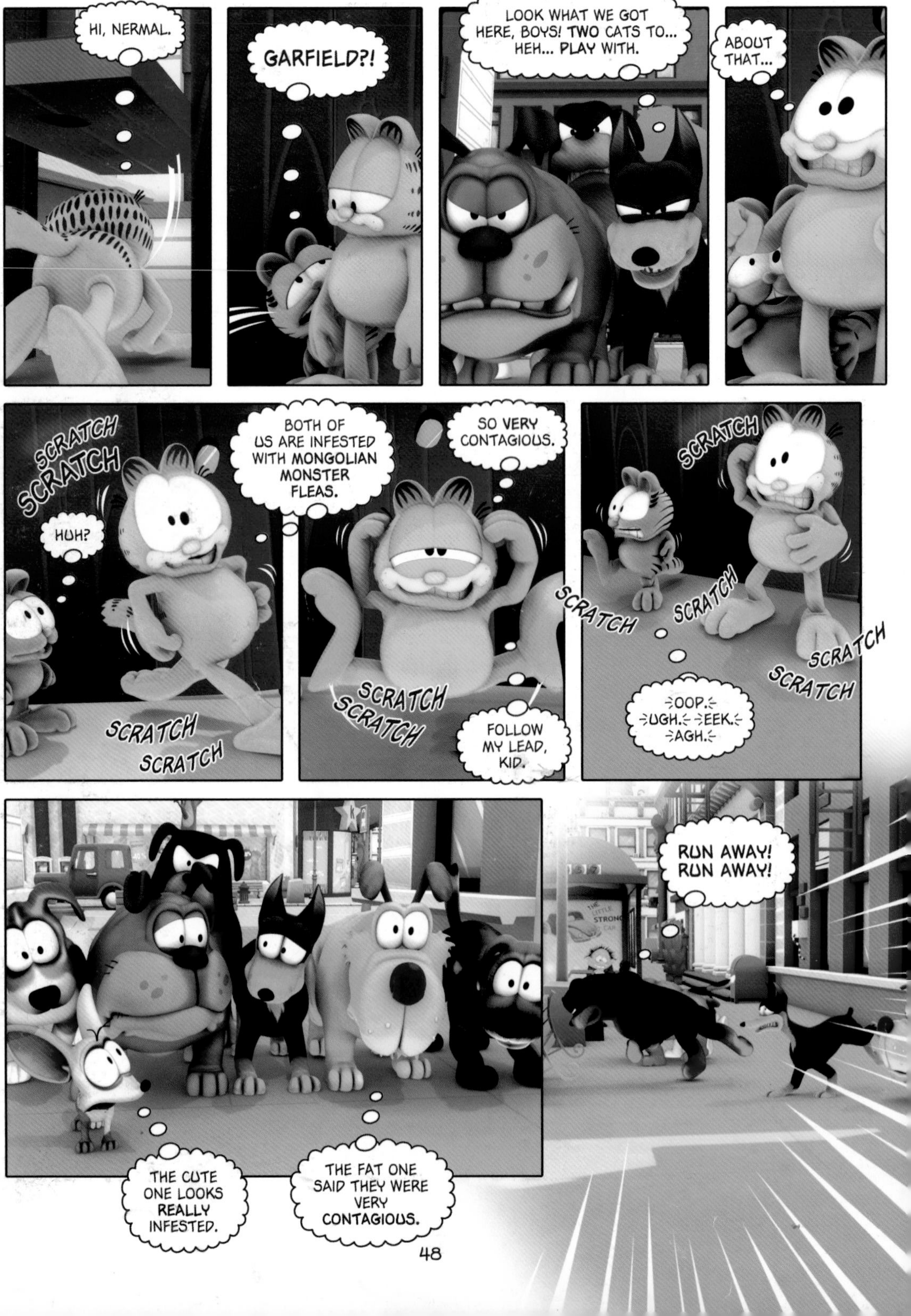
HI, NERMAL.
GARFIELD?!
LOOK WHAT WE GOT HERE, BOYS! TWO CATS TO... HEH... PLAY WITH.
ABOUT THAT...
SCRATCH SCRATCH
HUH?
BOTH OF US ARE INFESTED WITH MONGOLIAN MONSTER FLEAS.
SCRATCH SCRATCH
SO VERY CONTAGIOUS.
SCRATCH SCRATCH
FOLLOW MY LEAD, KID.
SCRATCH
SCRATCH
SCRATCH
SCRATCH
OOP. UGH. EEK. AGH.
THE CUTE ONE LOOKS REALLY INFESTED.
THE FAT ONE SAID THEY WERE VERY CONTAGIOUS.
RUN AWAY! RUN AWAY!

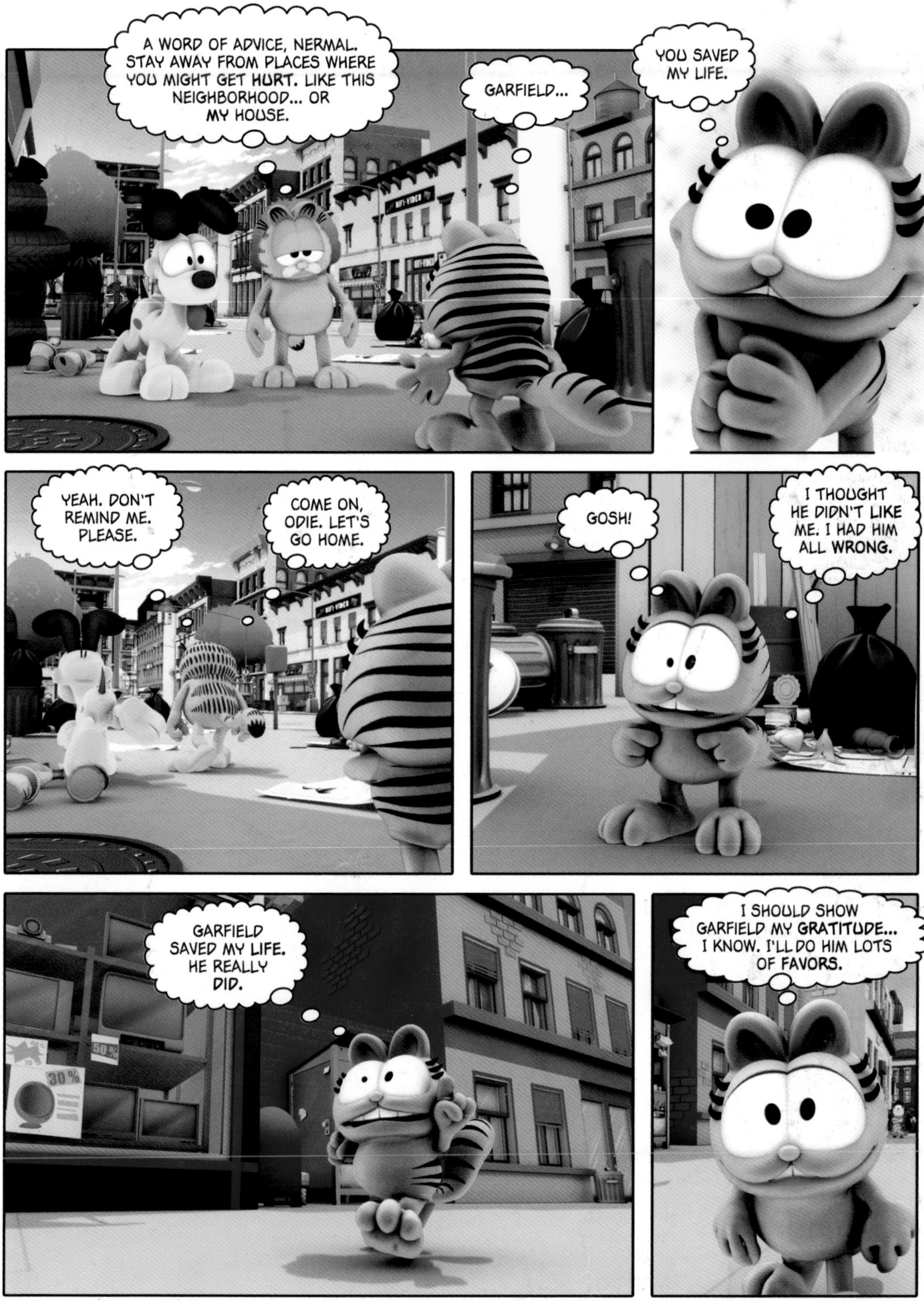
A WORD OF ADVICE, NERMAL. STAY AWAY FROM PLACES WHERE YOU MIGHT GET HURT. LIKE THIS NEIGHBORHOOD... OR MY HOUSE.
GARFIELD...
YOU SAVED MY LIFE.
YEAH. DON'T REMIND ME. PLEASE.
COME ON, ODIE. LET'S GO HOME.
GOSH!
I THOUGHT HE DIDN'T LIKE ME. I HAD HIM ALL WRONG.
GARFIELD SAVED MY LIFE. HE REALLY DID.
I SHOULD SHOW GARFIELD MY GRATITUDE... I KNOW. I'LL DO HIM LOTS OF FAVORS.

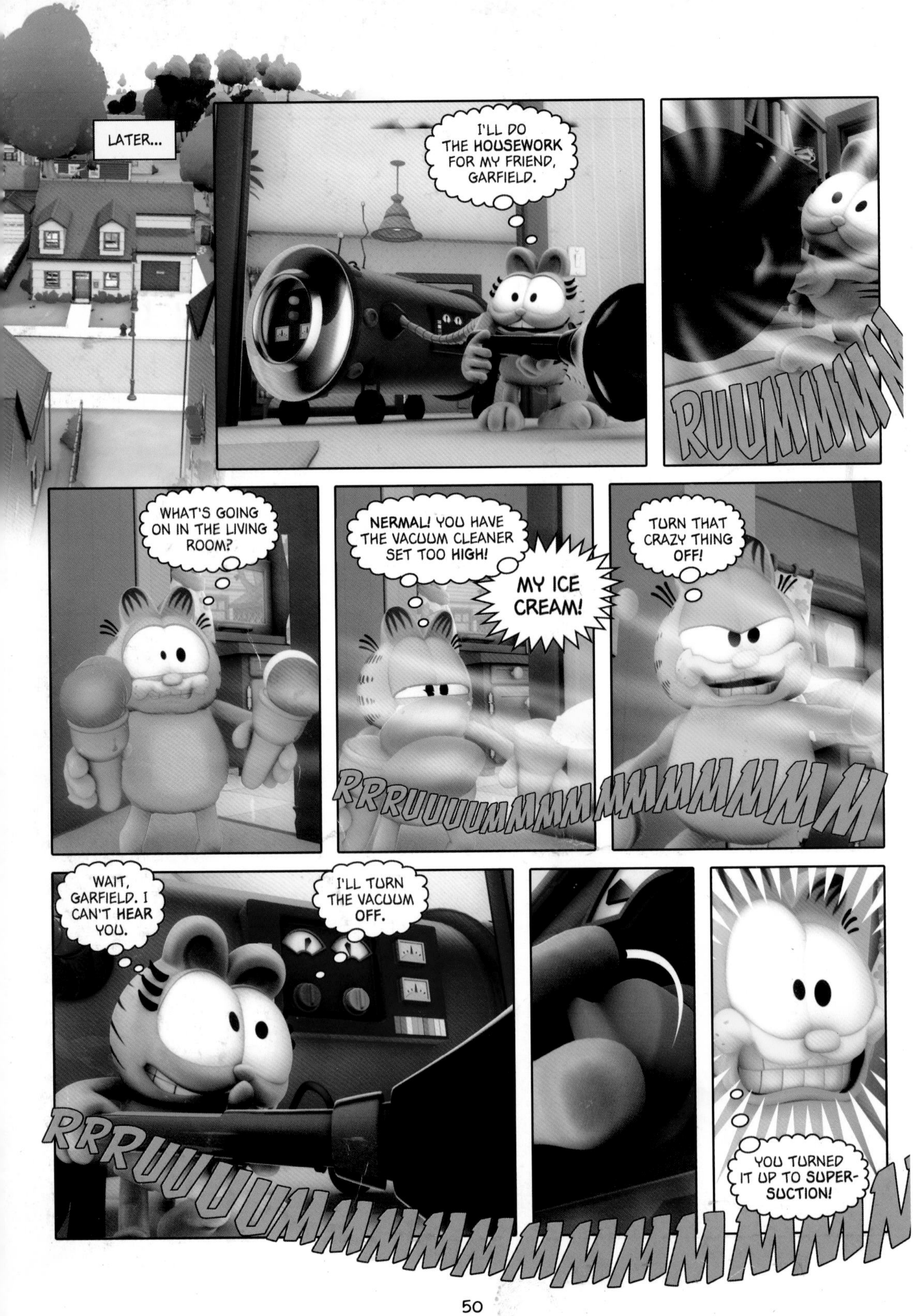
LATER...
I'LL DO THE HOUSEWORK FOR MY FRIEND, GARFIELD.
RUUMMMM
WHAT'S GOING ON IN THE LIVING ROOM?
NERMAL! YOU HAVE THE VACUUM CLEANER SET TOO HIGH!
MY ICE CREAM!
TURN THAT CRAZY THING OFF!
RRRUUUUMMMMMMMMMMMMMMMM
WAIT, GARFIELD. I CAN'T HEAR YOU.
I'LL TURN THE VACUUM OFF.
YOU TURNED IT UP TO SUPER-SUCTION!
RRRUUUUMMMMMMMMMMMMMMMMN

WAAAAAAAAH!

SORRY, SORRY, SORRY...

PRRUUUUMMMMMMMMMMMMMMMMMMMMMMMMMMMMM

GARFIELD. LIZ IS COMING TO VISIT TONIGHT.

WE NEED TO CLEAN UP THE LIVING--

WHAT...?!

GARFIELD! WHAT HAVE YOU DONE?

IT WASN'T ME. IT WAS NERMAL!

I SAW MY LIFE FLASH BEFORE MY EYES.

AND THERE WAS LASAGNA.

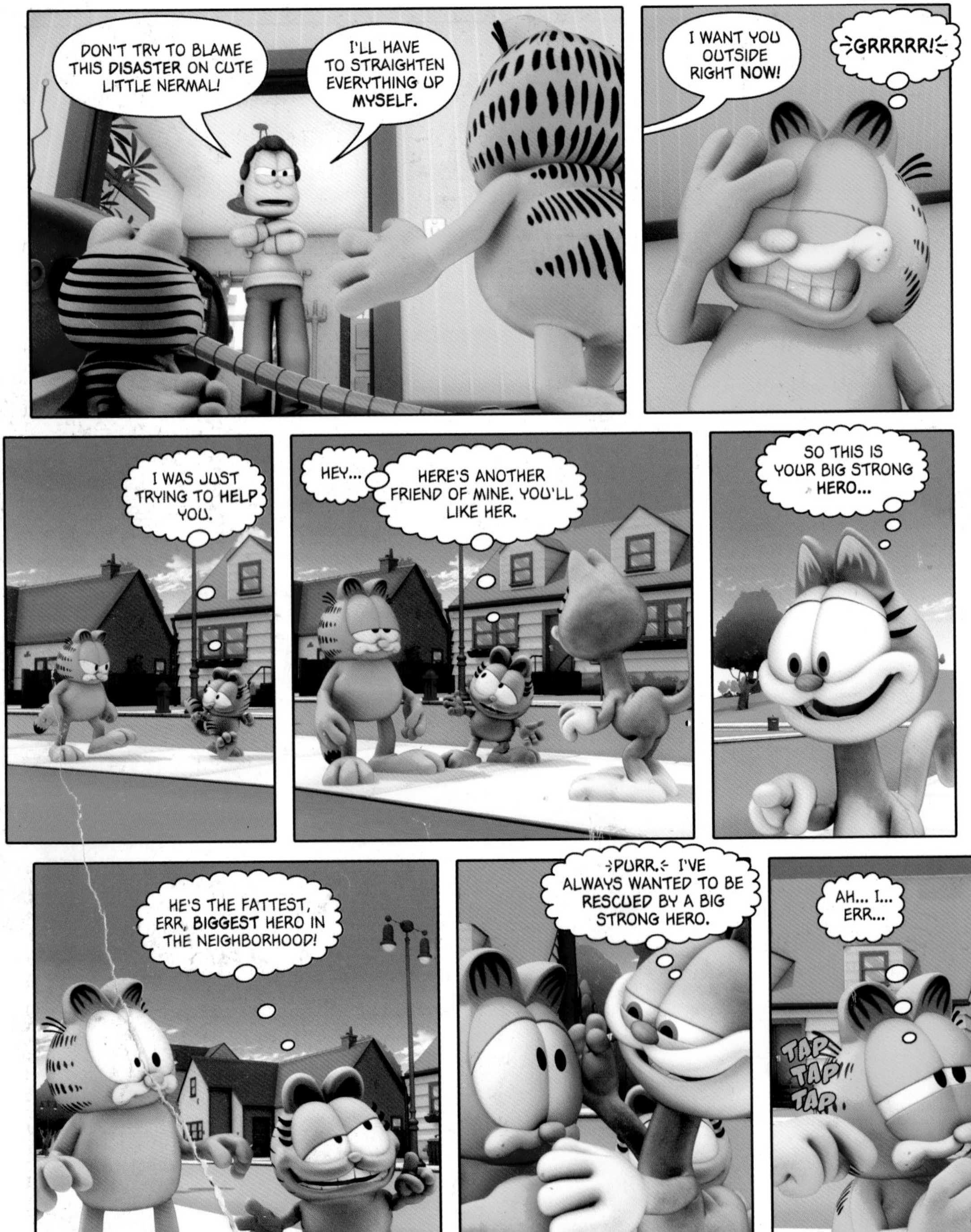
DON'T TRY TO BLAME THIS DISASTER ON CUTE LITTLE NERMAL!
I'LL HAVE TO STRAIGHTEN EVERYTHING UP MYSELF.
I WANT YOU OUTSIDE RIGHT NOW!
GRRRRR!
I WAS JUST TRYING TO HELP YOU.
HEY...
HERE'S ANOTHER FRIEND OF MINE. YOU'LL LIKE HER.
SO THIS IS YOUR BIG STRONG HERO...
HE'S THE FATTEST, ERR, BIGGEST HERO IN THE NEIGHBORHOOD!
PURR. I'VE ALWAYS WANTED TO BE RESCUED BY A BIG STRONG HERO.
AH... I... ERR...
TAP TAP TAP

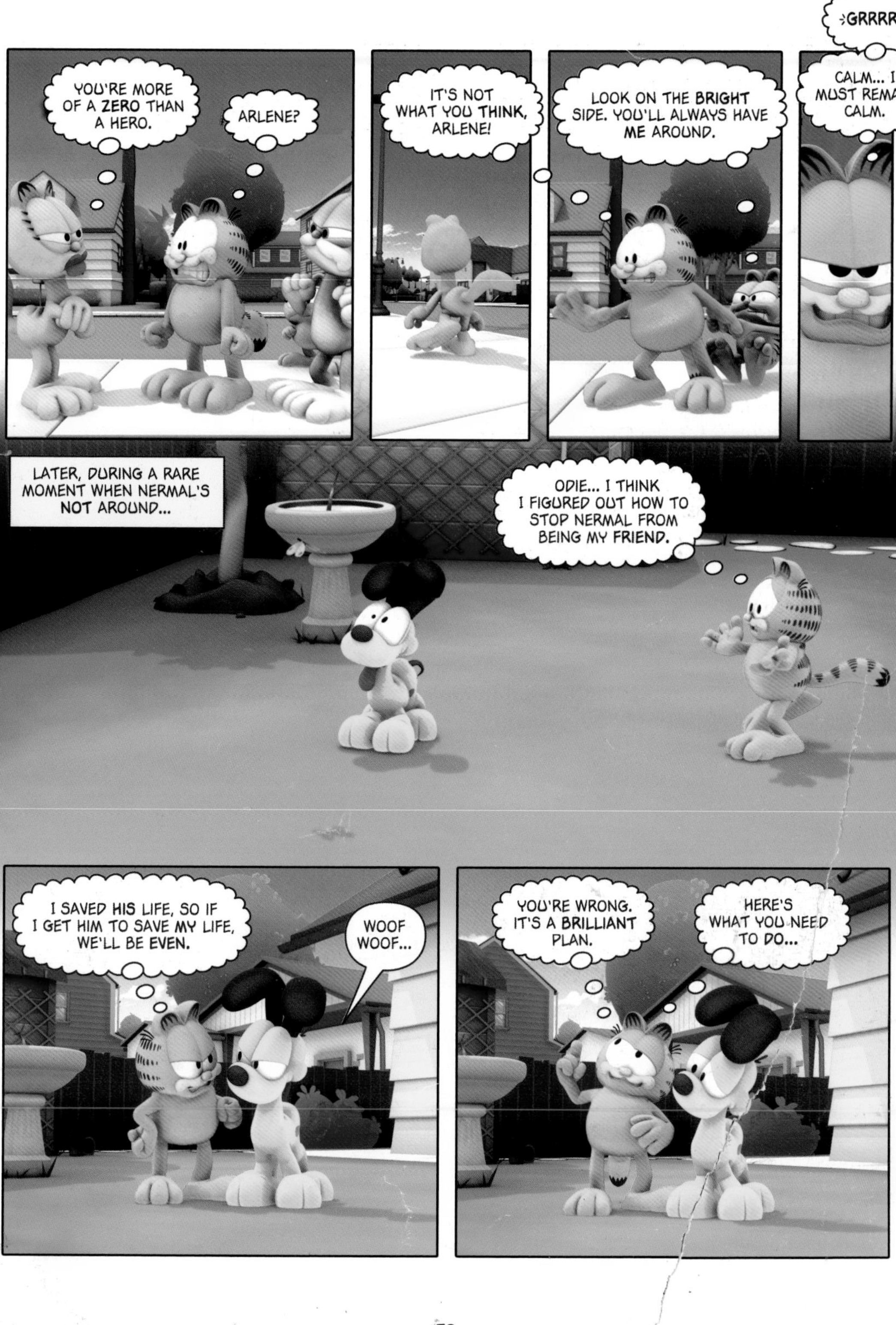
YOU'RE MORE OF A ZERO THAN A HERO.
ARLENE?
IT'S NOT WHAT YOU THINK, ARLENE!
LOOK ON THE BRIGHT SIDE. YOU'LL ALWAYS HAVE ME AROUND.
GRRRRR!
CALM... I MUST REMAIN CALM.
LATER, DURING A RARE MOMENT WHEN NERMAL'S NOT AROUND...
ODIE... I THINK I FIGURED OUT HOW TO STOP NERMAL FROM BEING MY FRIEND.
I SAVED HIS LIFE, SO IF I GET HIM TO SAVE MY LIFE, WE'LL BE EVEN.
WOOF WOOF...
YOU'RE WRONG. IT'S A BRILLIANT PLAN.
HERE'S WHAT YOU NEED TO DO...

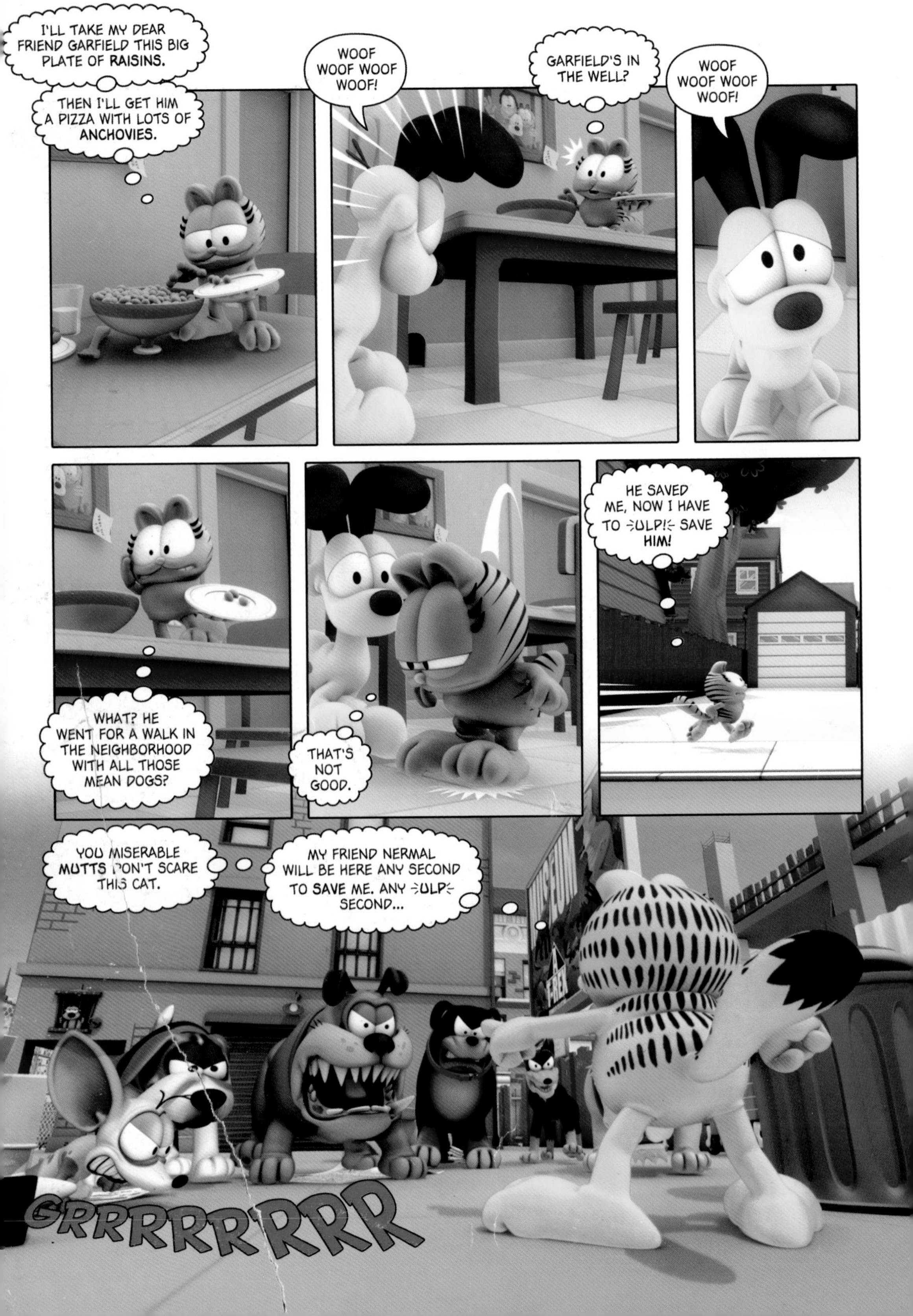

I'LL TAKE MY DEAR FRIEND GARFIELD THIS BIG PLATE OF **RAISINS.**
THEN I'LL GET HIM A PIZZA WITH LOTS OF **ANCHOVIES.**
WOOF WOOF WOOF WOOF!
GARFIELD'S IN THE WELL?
WOOF WOOF WOOF WOOF!
WHAT? HE WENT FOR A WALK IN THE NEIGHBORHOOD WITH ALL THOSE MEAN DOGS?
THAT'S NOT GOOD.
HE SAVED ME, NOW I HAVE TO ULP! SAVE **HIM!**
YOU MISERABLE **MUTTS** DON'T SCARE THIS CAT.
MY FRIEND NERMAL WILL BE HERE ANY SECOND TO **SAVE** ME. ANY ULP SECOND...
GRRRRRRRR

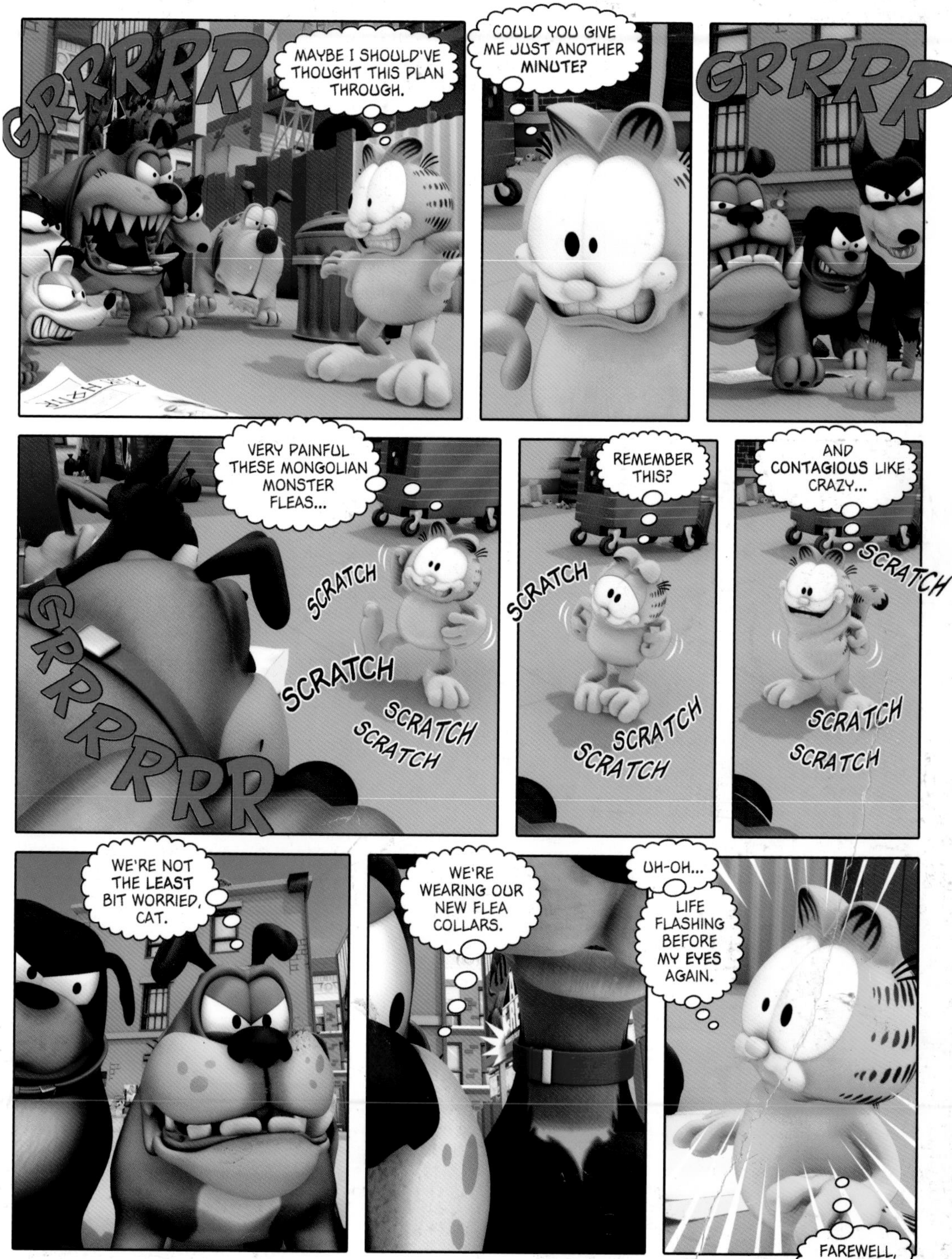
GRRRRR
MAYBE I SHOULD'VE THOUGHT THIS PLAN THROUGH.
COULD YOU GIVE ME JUST ANOTHER MINUTE?
GRRRRR
VERY PAINFUL THESE MONGOLIAN MONSTER FLEAS...
GRRRRRR
SCRATCH
SCRATCH
SCRATCH
SCRATCH
REMEMBER THIS?
SCRATCH
SCRATCH
SCRATCH
AND CONTAGIOUS LIKE CRAZY...
SCRATCH
SCRATCH
SCRATCH
WE'RE NOT THE LEAST BIT WORRIED, CAT.
WE'RE WEARING OUR NEW FLEA COLLARS.
UH-OH...
LIFE FLASHING BEFORE MY EYES AGAIN.
FAREWELL, LASAGNA...

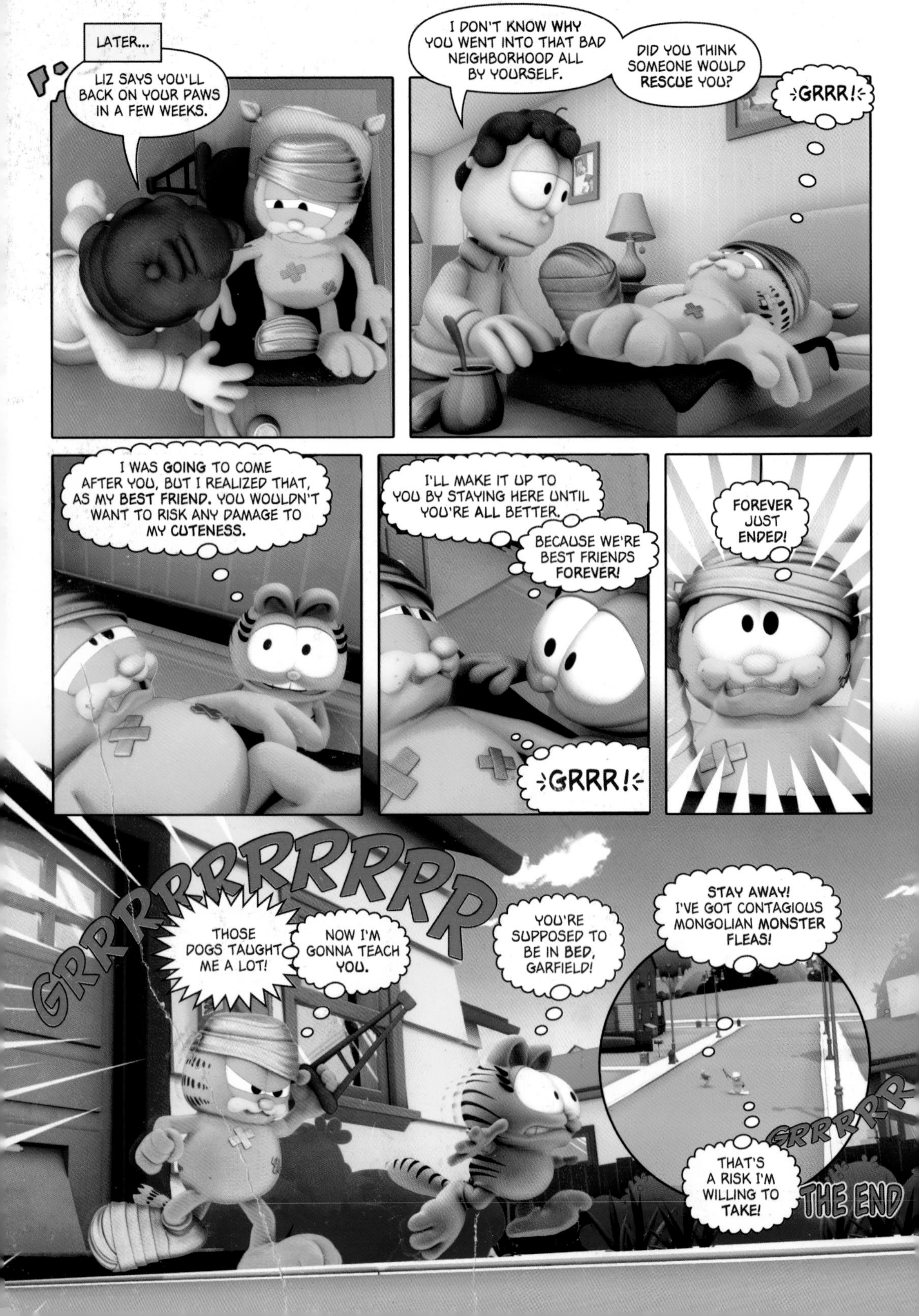

LATER...
LIZ SAYS YOU'LL BACK ON YOUR PAWS IN A FEW WEEKS.
I DON'T KNOW WHY YOU WENT INTO THAT BAD NEIGHBORHOOD ALL BY YOURSELF.
DID YOU THINK SOMEONE WOULD RESCUE YOU?
GRRR!
I WAS GOING TO COME AFTER YOU, BUT I REALIZED THAT, AS MY BEST FRIEND. YOU WOULDN'T WANT TO RISK ANY DAMAGE TO MY CUTENESS.
I'LL MAKE IT UP TO YOU BY STAYING HERE UNTIL YOU'RE ALL BETTER.
BECAUSE WE'RE BEST FRIENDS FOREVER!
GRRR!
FOREVER JUST ENDED!
GRRRRRRRRRRR
THOSE DOGS TAUGHT ME A LOT!
NOW I'M GONNA TEACH YOU.
YOU'RE SUPPOSED TO BE IN BED, GARFIELD!
STAY AWAY! I'VE GOT CONTAGIOUS MONGOLIAN MONSTER FLEAS!
GRRRRR
THAT'S A RISK I'M WILLING TO TAKE!
THE END

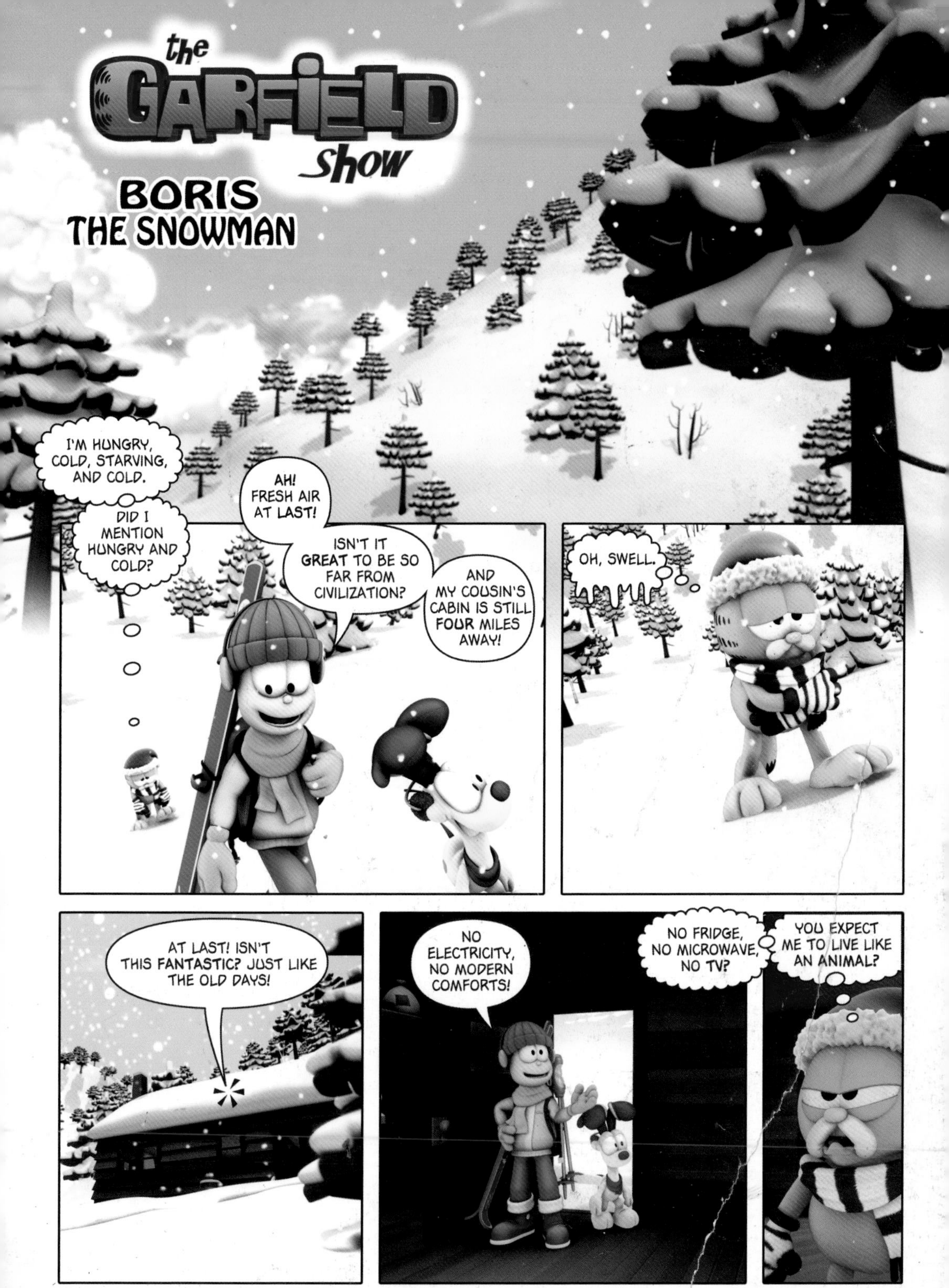
the GARFIELD show
BORIS THE SNOWMAN
I'M HUNGRY, COLD, STARVING, AND COLD.
DID I MENTION HUNGRY AND COLD?
AH! FRESH AIR AT LAST!
ISN'T IT GREAT TO BE SO FAR FROM CIVILIZATION?
AND MY COUSIN'S CABIN IS STILL FOUR MILES AWAY!
OH, SWELL.
AT LAST! ISN'T THIS FANTASTIC? JUST LIKE THE OLD DAYS!
NO ELECTRICITY, NO MODERN COMFORTS!
NO FRIDGE, NO MICROWAVE, NO TV?
YOU EXPECT ME TO LIVE LIKE AN ANIMAL?

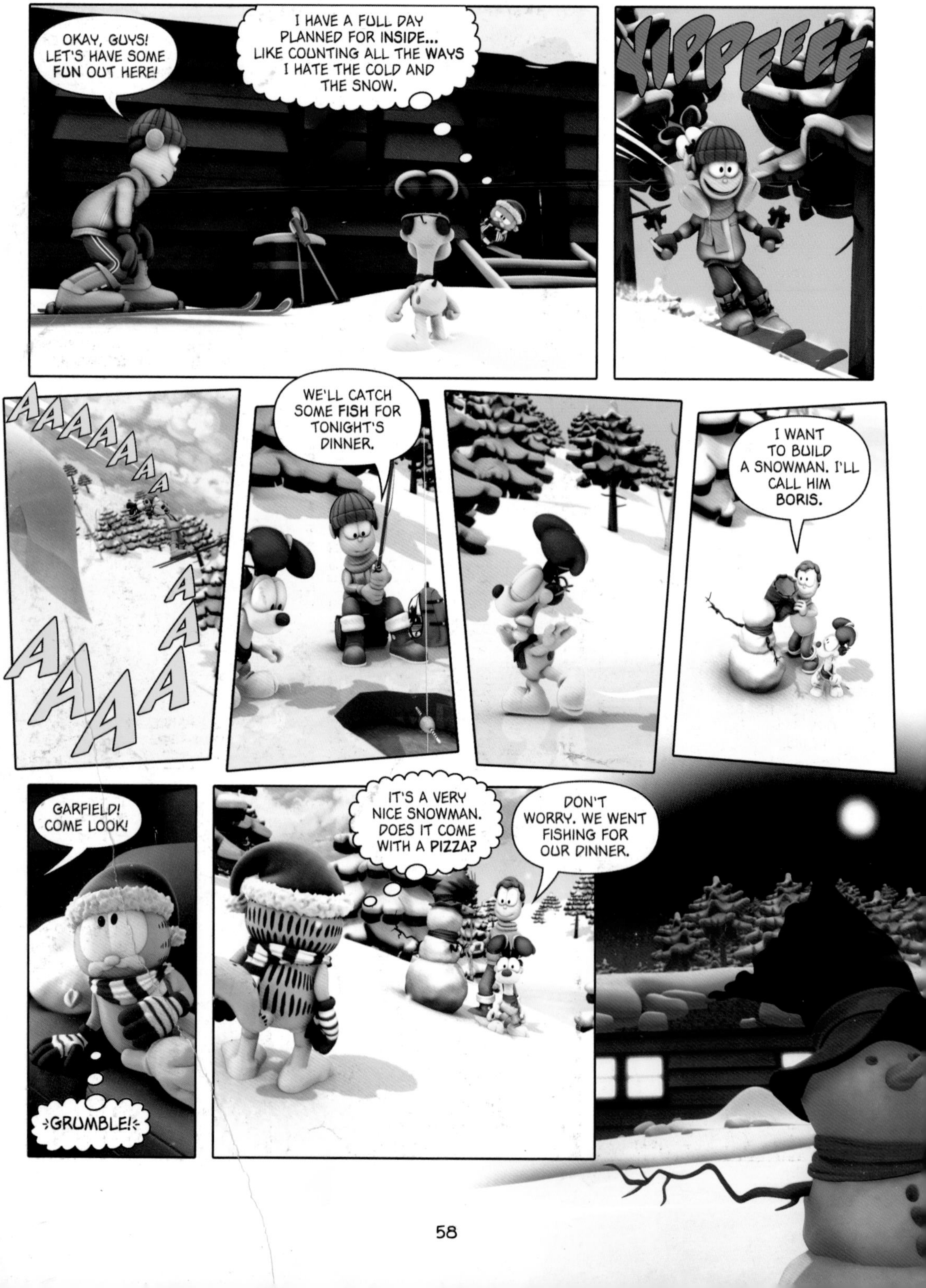
OKAY, GUYS! LET'S HAVE SOME FUN OUT HERE!
I HAVE A FULL DAY PLANNED FOR INSIDE... LIKE COUNTING ALL THE WAYS I HATE THE COLD AND THE SNOW.
YIPPEEEEE
AAAAAAAAAAAAAAAA
WE'LL CATCH SOME FISH FOR TONIGHT'S DINNER.
I WANT TO BUILD A SNOWMAN. I'LL CALL HIM BORIS.
GARFIELD! COME LOOK!
GRUMBLE!
IT'S A VERY NICE SNOWMAN. DOES IT COME WITH A PIZZA?
DON'T WORRY. WE WENT FISHING FOR OUR DINNER.

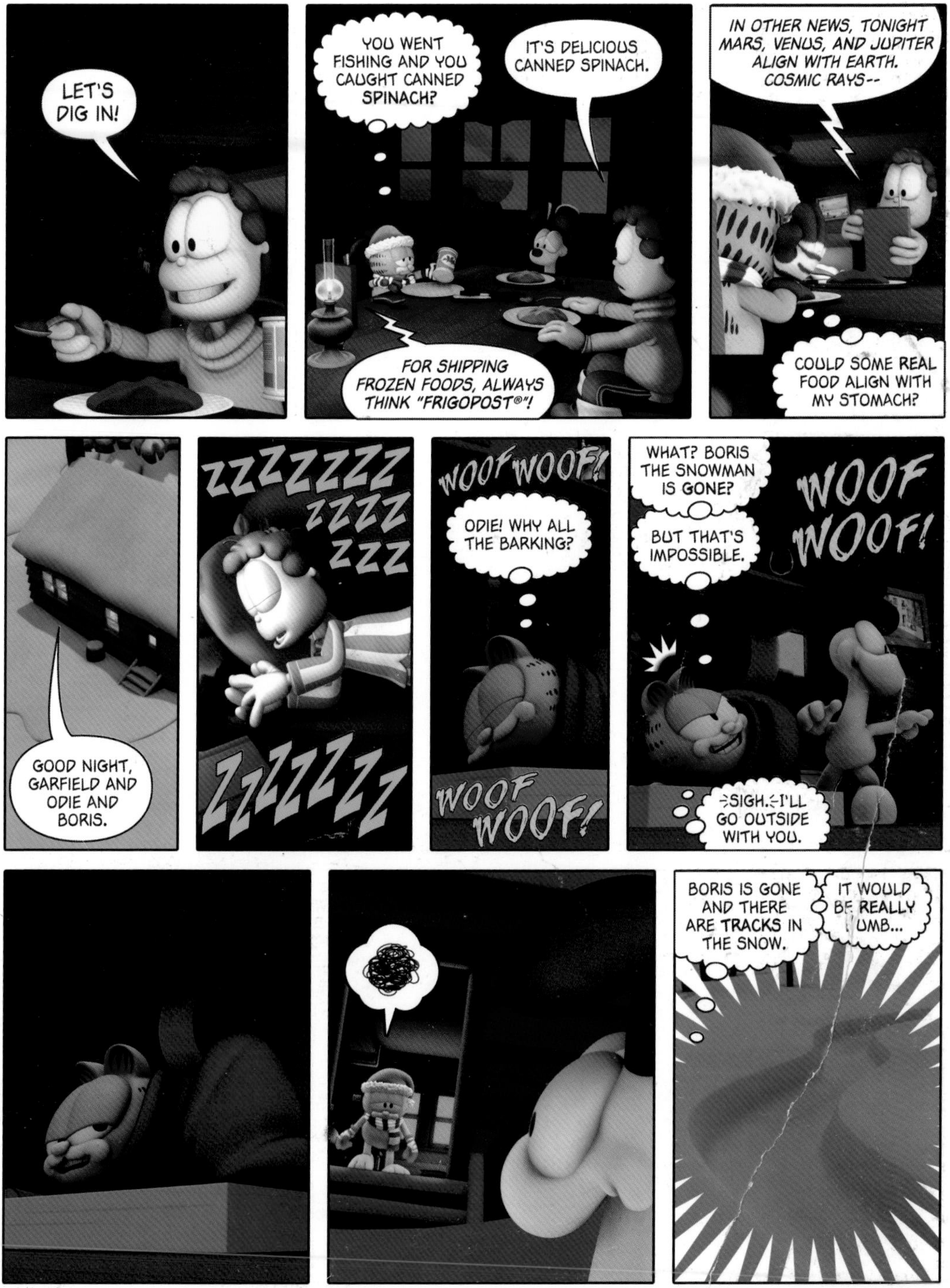

LET'S DIG IN!
YOU WENT FISHING AND YOU CAUGHT CANNED SPINACH?
IT'S DELICIOUS CANNED SPINACH.
FOR SHIPPING FROZEN FOODS, ALWAYS THINK "FRIGOPOST®"!
IN OTHER NEWS, TONIGHT MARS, VENUS, AND JUPITER ALIGN WITH EARTH. COSMIC RAYS--
COULD SOME REAL FOOD ALIGN WITH MY STOMACH?
GOOD NIGHT, GARFIELD AND ODIE AND BORIS.
ZZZZZZZ ZZZZ ZZZ
ZZZZZZZ
WOOF WOOF!
ODIE! WHY ALL THE BARKING?
WOOF WOOF!
WHAT? BORIS THE SNOWMAN IS GONE?
BUT THAT'S IMPOSSIBLE.
WOOF WOOF!
SIGH. I'LL GO OUTSIDE WITH YOU.
BORIS IS GONE AND THERE ARE TRACKS IN THE SNOW.
IT WOULD BE REALLY

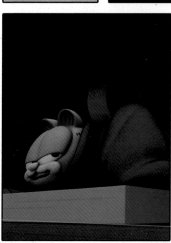

...TO FOLLOW THESE TRACKS INTO THE NIGHT.

DID WE LEARN NOTHING FROM HORROR MOVIES?

HEY, OLAF, HOW DO YOU KNOW WHEN A SNOWMAN IS SAD?

AND NOW WE'RE HEARING VOICES.

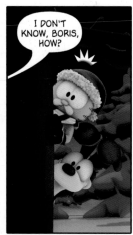

I DON'T KNOW, BORIS, HOW?

WHEN YOU SEE HIM CRY ICE CUBES!

HA HA HA! THAT'S COLD, BROTHER.

GOT ANY MORE?

AH... HELLO?

YOU...

YOU'RE REALLY TALKING?

OF COURSE!

IT'S CLASSIC REALLY. THREE PLANETS ALIGN WITH EARTH. WE GET HIT WITH COSMIC RAYS. NOW WE'RE ALIVE. JUST ROLL WITH IT.

NOW THAT YOU KNOW OUR SECRET, WHY NOT GET IN ON THE FUN?

OKAY. WHAT DO SNOWMEN CALL SNOWBALLS?

"CHILDREN."

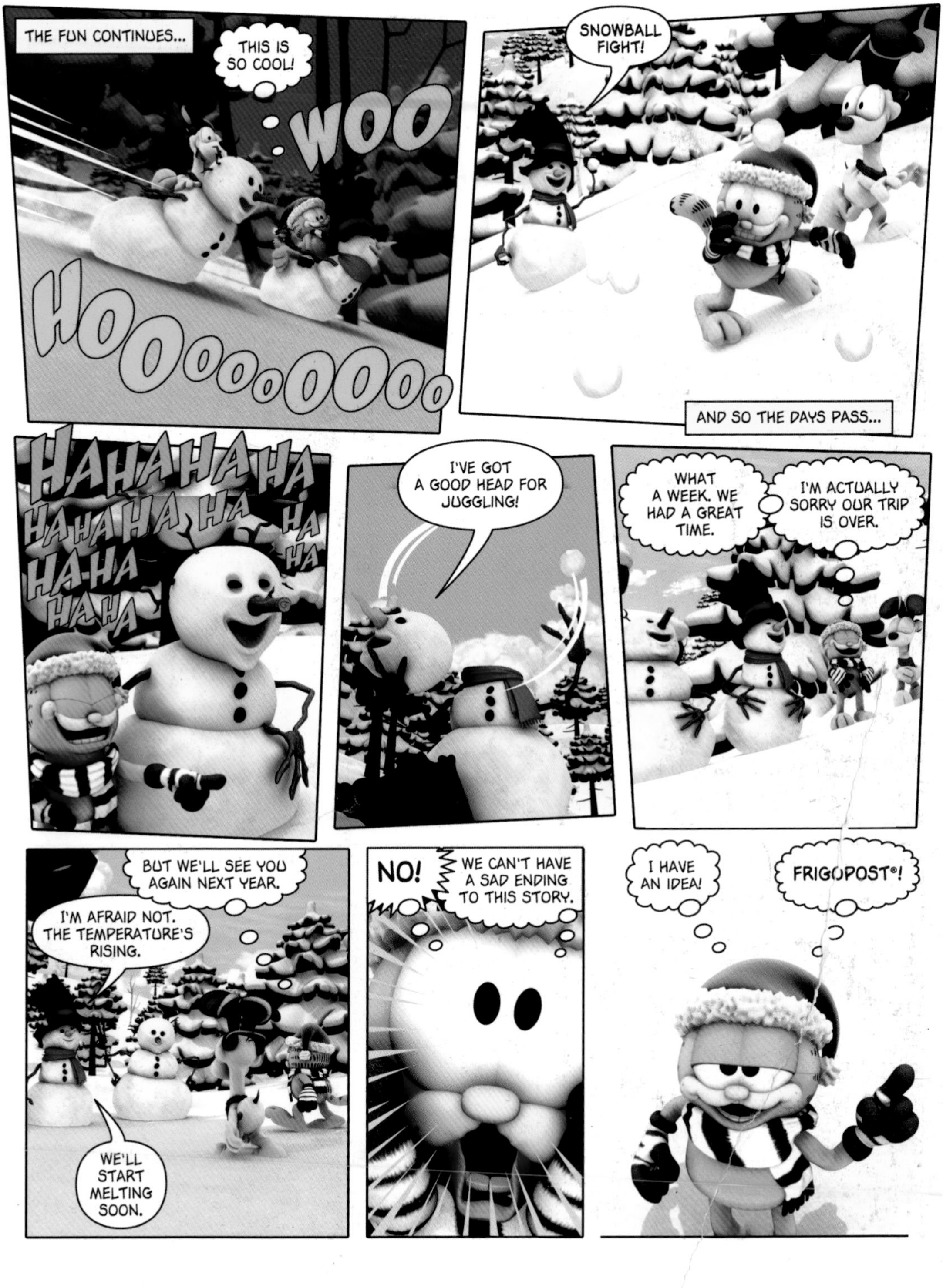
THE FUN CONTINUES...
THIS IS SO COOL!
WOO
HOOOOOOOOOO
SNOWBALL FIGHT!
AND SO THE DAYS PASS...
HAHAHAHAHA HAHAHA HA HA HAHA HAHA HA HA
I'VE GOT A GOOD HEAD FOR JUGGLING!
WHAT A WEEK. WE HAD A GREAT TIME.
I'M ACTUALLY SORRY OUR TRIP IS OVER.
BUT WE'LL SEE YOU AGAIN NEXT YEAR.
I'M AFRAID NOT. THE TEMPERATURE'S RISING.
WE'LL START MELTING SOON.
NO!
WE CAN'T HAVE A SAD ENDING TO THIS STORY.
I HAVE AN IDEA!
FRIGOPOST®!

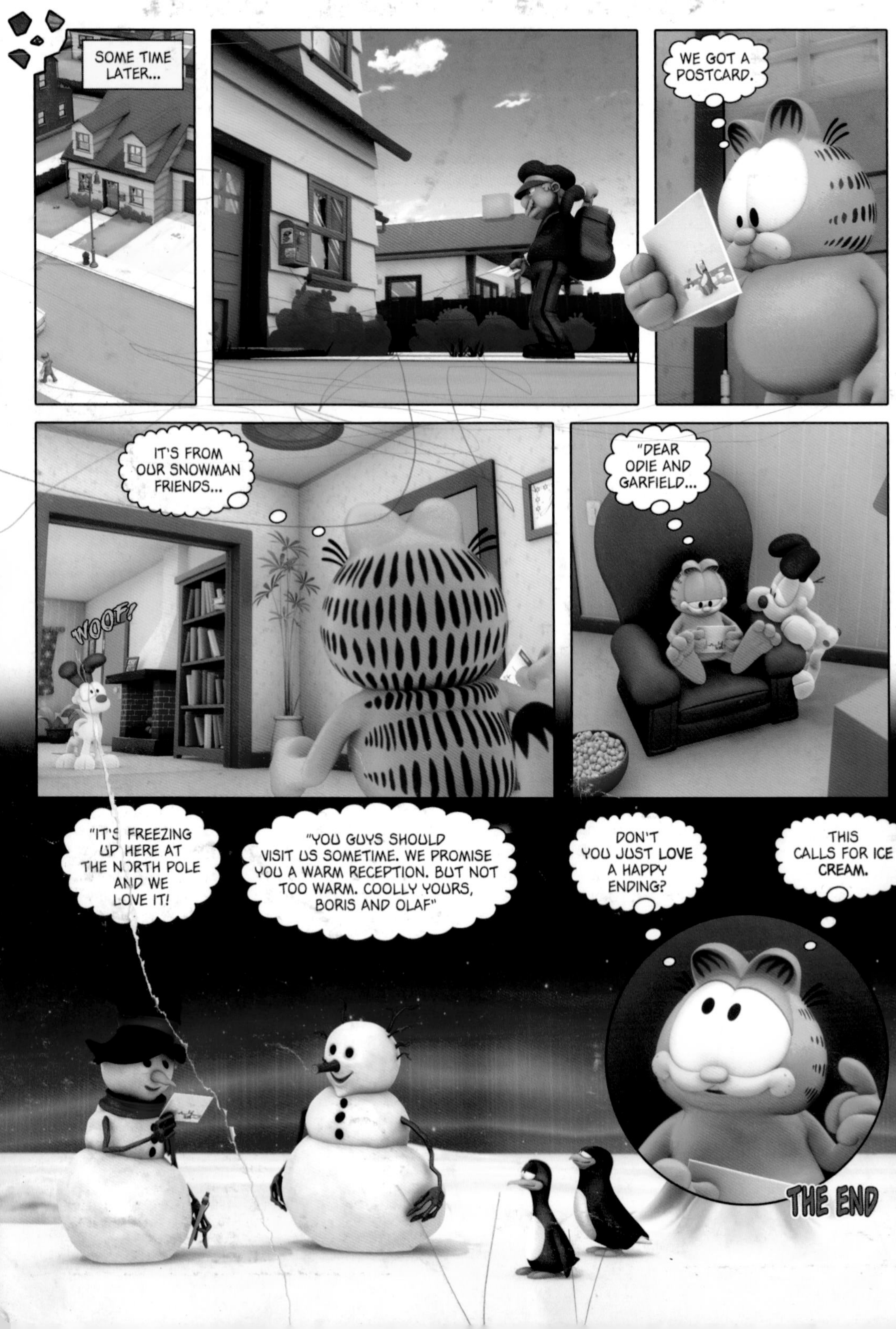
SOME TIME LATER...
WE GOT A POSTCARD.
IT'S FROM OUR SNOWMAN FRIENDS...
WOOF!
"DEAR ODIE AND GARFIELD...
"IT'S FREEZING UP HERE AT THE NORTH POLE AND WE LOVE IT!
"YOU GUYS SHOULD VISIT US SOMETIME. WE PROMISE YOU A WARM RECEPTION. BUT NOT TOO WARM. COOLLY YOURS, BORIS AND OLAF"
DON'T YOU JUST LOVE A HAPPY ENDING?
THIS CALLS FOR ICE CREAM.
THE END

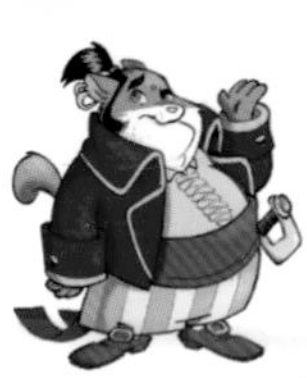

WATCH OUT FOR PAPERCUTZ™

Welcome to the fabulously furry fourth THE GARFIELD SHOW graphic novel from Papercutz, the cat-loving folks devoted to publishing great graphic novels for all ages. I'm Jim Salicrup, Editor-in-Chief and fellow lasagna aficionado, here to talk about a few other cartoon cats, cats we like to call THE PAPERCATZ...

While Garfield is certainly Top Cat, so to speak, at Papercutz, there certainly are a few other cartoon kitties populating the pages of several other Papercutz publications. You may even remember some of them from the quirky quiz we ran back in THE GARFIELD SHOW #2.

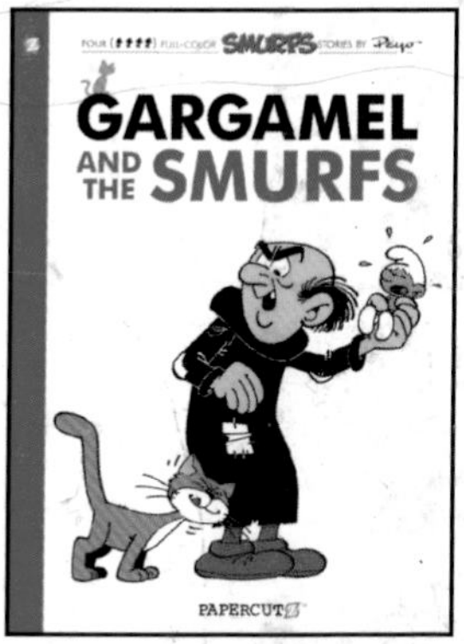
SMURFS
GARGAMEL AND THE SMURFS
PAPERCUTZ

The first is fairly well-known, as the pet of Gargamel, the evil wizard obsessed with making life difficult for our little blue buddies, THE SMURFS. Of course, we're talking about Azrael, perhaps the oldest cat currently running in our graphic novels. The Smurfs were created over 50 years ago by Pierre Culliford, better known as Peyo, and Azrael debuted right alongside Gargamel in the very first panel of "The Smurfnapper." Azrael isn't necessarily a bad cat, as I believe most cats would want to attack Smurfs if given the opportunity. Just like we can't choose our parents, Azrael didn't choose gargamel to be his owner. You can find this story in both THE SMURFS #9 "Gargamel and the Smurfs" and the first volume of the deluxe THE SMURFS ANTHOLOGY.

Believing in equal time, believe it or not, Papercutz actually publishes a couple of titles starring... mice! Yes, it's true. In GERONIMO STILTON, the adventures of the time-travelling Editor-in-Chief of New Mouse City's The Rodent's Gazette, who is perpetually saving the future, by protecting the past, the villains are the wicked Pirate Cats—Catardone III of Catatonia, Tersilla of catatonia, and Bonzo Felix (Yes, a cat named Felix!). Unlike Garfield, who long ago gave up the notion of battling mice, The Pirate Cats continually persist in trying to get the upper paw in their dealings with Geronimo and his family and friends. They even go so far as to disguise themselves as mice, but it's all to no avail. They never win.

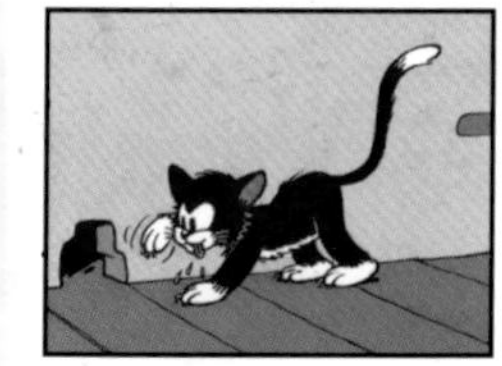

For the overly literal of you, you may be asking if Papercutz publishes two titles starring mice (GERONIMO STILTON and THEA STILTON) and only one starring a cat, how is that "equal time." Well, it's not. But we will soon be publishing another book by Peyo entitled PUSSYCAT, which will collect all of his cat comic strips in one volume. This cat actually came before Azrael, so he will soon be the oldest Papercutz cat. These strips have never before been collected or published in America until now. If you're curious, like a cat, and want to see the early work of the cartoonist who created THE SMURFS, this book is for you!

There are actually several more cats appearing in other Papercutz graphic novels, but we're actually running out of room, so maybe we should save the rest for THE GARFIELD SHOW #5?

Speaking of which, for those fans of great comicbook lettering are wondering what happened to Tom Orzechowski (I said he'd be back in this book), he had to take some time off to move from California to Ohio. He'll be back in THE GARFIELD SHOW #5, but we wanted to thank the wonderful Janice Chiang for filling in for him! So, let's all do this again (except you, Janice), when we return in THE GARFIELD SHOW #5!

Thanks,

JIM

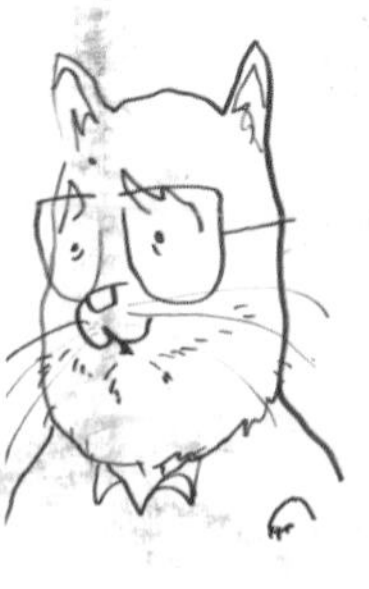

STAY IN TOUCH!

EMAIL:	SALICRUP@PAPERCUTZ.COM
WEB:	PAPERCUTZ.COM
TWITTER:	@PAPERCUTZGN
FACEBOOK:	PAPERCUTZGRAPHICNOVELS
BIRTHDAY CARDS:	PAPERCUTZ, 160 BROADWAY, SUITE 700, EAST WING, NEW YORK, NY 10038

More Great Graphic Novels from PAPERCUTZ™

Tinker Bell
and the Secret of the Wings
PAPERCUTZ

DISNEY FAIRIES #15

"Tinker Bell and the Secret of the Wings"

The hit DVD in comics!

Guillaume Bianco
Antonello Dalena
Ernest & Rebecca

ERNEST & REBECCA #5

"The School of Nonsense"

A 6 ½ year old girl and her microbial buddy against the world!

MIGHTY MORPHIN
POWER RANGERS
PAPERCUTZ

MIGHTY MORPHIN POWER RANGERS #2

"Going Green"

The Green Ranger's origins: revealed!

Blue Sky Studios
RIO
SNAKES ALIVE!
PAPERCUTZ

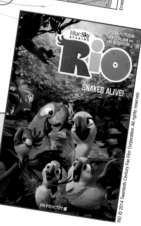

RIO #1

"Snakes Alive!"

An all-new, exclusive prequel to RIO 2 that takes place after the original hit RIO film!

SMURFS
THE SMURF ACCOUNTANT
PAPERCUTZ

THE SMURFS #18

"The Smurf Accountant"

More money, more problems in the Smurf's Village!

SYBIL
the Backpack Fairy
"Princess Nina"
PAPERCUTZ

SYBIL THE BACKPACK FAIRY #4

"Princess Nina"

Nina and Sybil's Excellent Adventure Through Time!

Available at better booksellers everywhere!

Or order directly from us! DISNEY FAIRIES is available in paperback for $7.99, in hardcover for $11.99; ERNEST & REBECCA is $11.99 in hardcover only; MIGHTY MORPHIN POWER RANGERS is available in paperback for $7.99, in hardcover for $12.99; RIO is available in paperback for $7.99 each, in hardcover for $11.99; THE SMURFS are available in paperback for $5.99, in hardcover for $10.99; and SYBIL THE BACKPACK FAIRY is available in hardcover only for $10.99.

Please add $4.00 for postage and handling for the first book, add $1.00 for each additional book.

Please make check payable to NBM Publishing. Send to: PAPERCUTZ, 160 Broadway, Suite 700, East Wing, New York, NY 10038

(1-800-886-1223)

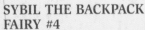